No one can resist a book by Diana Palmer!

"Nobody does it better."
—*New York Times* bestselling author Linda Howard

"Palmer knows how to make the sparks fly....
Heartwarming."
—*Publishers Weekly* on *Renegade*

"A compelling tale...
[that packs] an emotional wallop."
—*Booklist* on *Renegade*

"Sensual and suspenseful."
—*Booklist* on *Lawless*

"Diana Palmer is a mesmerizing storyteller who
captures the essence of what a romance should be."
—*Affaire de Coeur*

"Nobody tops Diana Palmer
when it comes to delivering pure,
undiluted romance. I love her stories."
—*New York Times* bestselling author
Jayne Ann Krentz

"The dialogue is charming,
the characters likable and the sex sizzling."
—*Publishers Weekly* on *Once in Paris*

Dear Reader,

Of all the characters I have created over the past thirty years, Harley Fowler has been the most complex. He started life in *Mercenary's Woman* as a cowboy who worked for mercenary Eb Scott's friend, the enigmatic Cy Parks. He was a braggart, a blowhard and a pain in the neck, but we got glimpses of the man he might become. In *The Winter Soldier,* he grew up. When confronted by violent drug dealers, he discovered that while he was pretending to be a professional soldier, Cy Parks, his reclusive boss, was the real article. Harley swallowed his pride and walked bravely into gunfire beside Cy Parks, Micah Steele and Eb Scott to take down a dangerous drug distribution center.

I have had many readers ask for Harley's own book, but until now I hadn't found just the right venue for him. Sometimes if you rush a story into publication, you do damage to the character it is intended to spotlight. I waited until I was certain I had the right story for Harley. Now, I am.

I hope all of you who wanted to know more about Cy Parks's mysterious foreman will be pleased at the revelations. As you might notice, this book is the beginning of a murder mystery that will unravel in subsequent books, most notably in the hardcover story of Kilraven and Winnie Sinclair next summer and in the following year's hardcover about Kilraven's half brother, Jon Blackhawk. Don't be impatient. It's going to be a good ride. I promise.

Love to all of you from your biggest fan,

Diana Palmer

DIANA PALMER

THE MAVERICK

Published by Silhouette Books
America's Publisher of Contemporary Romance

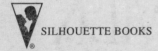 SILHOUETTE BOOKS

Recycling programs
for this product may
not exist in your area.

ISBN-13: 978-0-373-76982-7

THE MAVERICK

Copyright © 2009 by Diana Palmer

Visit Silhouette Books at www.eHarlequin.com

Printed in U.S.A.

DIANA PALMER

has a gift for telling the most sensual tales with charm and humor. With more than forty million copies of her books in print, Diana Palmer is one of North America's most beloved authors and considered one of the top ten romance authors in the United States.

Diana's hobbies include gardening, archaeology, anthropology, art, astronomy and music. She has been married to James Kyle for over thirty-five years. They have one son, Blayne, who is married to the former Christina Clayton, and a granddaughter, Selena Marie.

To Julie Benefiel, who designed my cowboy quilt
(hand pieced by Nancy Caudill),

To Nancy Mason, who quilted it,

And to Janet Borchert, who put together a 2007
hardcover book of all my covers, including foreign ones,
along with Jade, Tracy, Nancy, Carey, Amy, Renata,
Maria, LeeAnn, Efy, Kay, Peggy, Hang, Ronnie, Mona
and Debbie of the Diana Palmer Bulletin Board.

Also to everyone who participated in the compendium
summaries of all my books, and to Nancy for the
quilted covers for the loose-leaf notebooks.

With many thanks and much love.

One

Harley Fowler was staring so hard at his list of chores that he walked right into a young brunette as he headed into the hardware store in Jacobsville, Texas. He looked up, shocked, when she fell back against the open door, glaring at him.

"I've heard of men getting buried in their work, but this is too much," she told him with a speaking look. She smoothed over her short black hair, feeling for a bump where she'd collided with the door. Deep blue eyes glared up into his pale blue ones. She noticed that he had light brown hair and was wearing a baseball cap that seemed to suit him. He was sexy-looking.

"I'm not buried in my work," he said curtly. "I'm trying to get back to work, and shopping chores are keeping me from it."

"Which doesn't explain why you're assaulting women with doors. Does it?" she mused.

His eyes flared. "I didn't assault you with a door. You walked into me."

"I did not. You were staring at that piece of paper so hard that you wouldn't have seen a freight train coming." She peered over his arm at the list. "Pruning shears? Two new rakes?" She pursed her lips, but smiling blue eyes stared at him. "You're obviously somebody's gardener," she said, noting his muddy shoes and baseball cap.

His eyebrows met. "I am not a gardener," he said indignantly. "I'm a cowboy."

"You are not!"

"Excuse me?"

"You don't have a horse, you're not wearing a cowboy hat, and you don't have on any chaps." She glanced at his feet. "You aren't even wearing cowboy boots!"

He gaped at her. "Did you just escape from intense therapy?"

"I have not been in any therapy," she said haughtily. "My idiosyncrasies are so unique that they couldn't classify me even with the latest edition of the DSM-IV, much less attempt to pyschoanalize me!"

She was referring to a classic volume of psychology that was used to diagnose those with mental challenges. He obviously had no idea what she was talking about.

"So, can you sing, then?"

He looked hunted. "Why would I want to sing?"

"Cowboys sing. I read it in a book."

"You can read?" he asked in mock surprise.

"Why would you think I couldn't?" she asked.

He nodded toward the sign on the hardware store's door that clearly said, in large letters, PULL. She was trying to push it.

She let go of the door and shifted her feet. "I saw that," she said defensively. "I just wanted to know if you were paying attention." She cocked her head at him. "Do you have a rope?"

"Why?" he asked. "You planning to hang yourself?"

She sighed with exaggerated patience. "Cowboys carry ropes."

"What for?"

"So they can rope cattle!"

"Don't find many head of cattle wandering around in hardware stores," he murmured, looking more confident now.

"What if you did?" she persisted. "How would you get a cow out of the store?"

"Bull. We run purebred Santa Gertrudis bulls on Mr. Parks's ranch," he corrected.

"And you don't have any cows?" She made a face. "You don't raise calves, then." She nodded.

His face flamed. "We do so raise calves. We do have cows. We just don't carry them into hardware stores and turn them loose!"

"Well, excuse me!" she said in mock apology. "I never said you did."

"Cowboy hats and ropes and cows," he muttered. He opened the door. "You going in or standing out here? I have work to do."

"Doing what? Knocking unsuspecting women in the head with doors?" she asked pleasantly.

His impatient eyes went over her neat slacks and wool jacket, to the bag she was holding. "I said, are you going into the store?" he asked with forced patience, holding the door open.

"Yes, as a matter of fact, I am," she replied, moving closer. "I need some tape measures and Super Glue and matches and chalk and push pins and colored string and sticky tape."

"Don't tell me," he drawled. "You're a contractor."

"Oh, she's something a little less conventional than that, Harley," Police Chief Cash Grier said as he came up the steps to the store. "How's it going, Jones?" he asked.

"I'm overflowing in DBs, Grier," she replied with a grin. "Want some?"

He held up his hands. "We don't do a big business in homicides here. I'd like to keep it that way." He scowled. "You're out of your territory a bit, aren't you?"

"I am. I was asked down here by your sheriff, Hayes Carson. He actually does have a DB. I'm working the crime scene for him per his request through the Bexar County medical examiner's office, but I didn't bring enough supplies. I hope the hardware store can accommodate me. It's a long drive back to San Antonio when you're on a case."

"On a case?" Harley asked, confused.

"Yes, on a case," she said. "Unlike you, some of us are professionals who have real jobs."

"Do you know him?" Cash asked her.

She gave Harley a studied appraisal. "Not really. He came barreling up the steps and hit me with a door. He says he's a cowboy," she added in a confidential tone. "But just between us, I'm sure he's lying. He doesn't have a horse or a rope, he isn't wearing a cowboy hat or boots, he says he can't sing, and he thinks bulls roam around loose in hardware stores."

Harley stared at her with more mixed emotions than he'd felt in years.

Cash choked back a laugh. "Well, he actually is a cowboy," Cash defended him. "He's Harley Fowler, Cy Parks's foreman on his cattle ranch."

"Imagine that!" she exclaimed. "What a blow to the image of Texas if some tourist walks in and sees him dressed like that!" She indicated Harley's attire with one slender hand. "They can't call us the cowboy capital of the world if we have people working cattle in baseball caps! We'll be disgraced!"

Cash was trying not to laugh. Harley looked as if he might explode.

"Better a horseless cowboy than a contractor with an attitude like yours!" Harley shot back, with glittery eyes. "I'm amazed that anybody around here would hire you to build something for them."

She gave him a superior look. "I don't build things. But I could if I wanted to."

"She really doesn't build things," Cash said. "Harley, this is Alice Mayfield Jones," he introduced. "She's a forensic investigator for the Bexar County medical examiner's office."

"She works with dead people?" Harley exclaimed, and moved back a step.

"Dead bodies," Alice returned, glaring at his obvious distaste. "DBs. And I'm damned good at my job. Ask him," she added, nodding toward Cash.

"She does have a reputation," Cash admitted. His dark eyes twinkled. "And a nickname. Old Jab-'Em-in-the-Liver Alice."

"You've been talking to Marc Brannon," she accused.

"You did help him solve a case, back when he was still a Texas Ranger," he pointed out.

"Now they've got this new guy, transferred up from Houston," she said on a sigh. "He's real hard going. No sense of humor." She gave him a wry look. "Kind of like you used to be, in the old days when you worked out of the San Antonio district attorney's office, Grier," she recalled. "A professional loner with a bad attitude."

"Oh, I've changed." He grinned. "A wife and child can turn the worst of us inside out."

She smiled. "No kidding? If I have time, I'd love to see that little girl everybody's talking about. Is she as pretty as her mama?"

He nodded. "Oh, yes. Every bit."

Harley pulled at his collar. "Could you stop talking about children, please?" he muttered. "I'll break out in hives."

"Allergic to small things, are you?" Alice chided.

"Allergic to the whole subject of marriage," he emphasized with a meaningful stare.

Her eyebrows arched. "I'm sorry, were you hoping I was going to ask you to marry me?" she replied pleasantly. "You're not bad-looking, I guess, but I have a very high standard for prospective bridegrooms. Frankly," she added with a quick appraisal, "if you were on sale in a groom shop, I can assure you that I wouldn't purchase you."

He stared at her as if he doubted his hearing. Cash Grier had to turn away. His face was going purple.

The hardware-store door opened and a tall, black-haired, taciturn man came out it. He frowned. "Jones? What the hell are you doing down here? They asked for Longfellow!"

She glared back. "Longfellow hid in the women's restroom and refused to come out," she said haughtily. "So they sent me. And why are you interested in Sheriff Carson's case? You're a fed."

Kilraven put his finger to his lips and looked around hastily to make sure nobody was listening. "I'm a policeman, working on the city force," he said curtly.

Alice held up both hands defensively. "Sorry! It's so hard to keep up with all these secrets!"

Kilraven glanced at his boss and back at Alice. "What secrets?"

"Well, there's the horseless cowboy there—" she pointed at Harley "—and the DB over on the Little Carmichael River…"

Kilraven's silver eyes widened. "On the river? I thought it was in town. Nobody told me!"

"I just did," Alice said. "But it's really a secret. I'm not supposed to tell anybody."

"I'm local law enforcement," Kilraven insisted. "You can tell me. Who is he?"

Alice gave him a bland look and propped a hand on her hip. "I only looked at him for two minutes before I realized I needed to get more investigative supplies. He's male and dead. He's got no ID, he's naked, and even his mother wouldn't recognize his face."

"Dental records…" Kilraven began.

"For those, you need identifiable teeth," Alice replied sweetly.

Harley was turning white.

She glanced at him. "Are you squeamish?" she asked hopefully. "Listen, I once examined this dead guy whose girlfriend caught him with a hooker. After she offed him, she cut off his… Where are you going?"

Harley was making a beeline for the interior of the hardware store.

"Bathroom, I imagine." Grier grinned at Kilraven, who chuckled.

"He works around cattle and he's squeamish?" Alice asked, delighted. "I'll bet he's a lot of fun when they round up the calves!"

"Not nice," Kilraven chided. "Everybody's got a weak spot, Jones. Even you."

"I have no weak spots," she assured him.

"No social life, either," Grier murmured. "I heard you tried to conduct a postmortem on a turkey in North Carolina during a murder investigation there."

"It met with fowl play," she said, straight-faced.

Both men chuckled.

"I have to get to work," she said, becoming serious. "This is a strange case. Nobody knows who this guy is or where he came from, and there was a serious attempt to make him unidentifiable. Even with DNA, when I can get a profile back from state—and don't hold your breath on the timetable—I don't know if we can identify him. If he has no criminal record, he won't be on file anywhere."

"At least we don't get many of these," Kilraven said quietly.

Jones smiled at him. "When are you coming back up to San Antonio?" she asked. "You solved the Pendleton kidnapping and helped wrap up the perps."

"Just a few loose ends to tie up," he said. He nodded at her and his boss. "I'll get back on patrol."

"Brady's wife made potato soup and real corn bread for lunch. Don't miss it."

"Not me, boss."

Alice stared after the handsome officer. "He's a dish. But isn't he overstaying his purpose down here?" she asked Cash.

He leaned down. "Winnie Sinclair works for the 911 center. Local gossip has it that he's sweet on her. That's why he's finding excuses not to leave."

Alice looked worried. "And he's dragging around a whole past that hardly anybody knows about. He's pretending it never happened."

"Maybe he has to."

She nodded. "It was bad. One of the worst cases I ever worked. Poor guy." She frowned. "They never solved it, you know. The perp is still out there, running around loose. It must have driven Kilraven and his brother, Jon Blackhawk, nuts, wondering if it was somebody they arrested, somebody with a grudge."

"Their father was an FBI agent in San Antonio, before he drank himself to death after the murders. Blackhawk still is," Cash replied thoughtfully. "Could have been a case any one of the three men worked, a perp getting even."

"It could," she agreed. "It must haunt the brothers. The guilt would be bad enough, but they wouldn't want to risk it happening again, to someone else they got involved with. They avoid women. Especially Kilraven."

"He wouldn't want to go through it again," Cash said.

"This Sinclair woman, how does she feel about Kilraven?"

Cash gave her a friendly smile. "I am not a gossip."

"Bull."

He laughed. "She's crazy about him. But she's very young."

"Age doesn't matter, in the long run," Alice said with

a faraway look in her eyes. "At least, sometimes." She opened the door. "See you around, Grier."

"You, too, Jones."

She walked into the hardware store. There at the counter was Harley, pale and out of sorts. He glared at her.

She held up both hands. "I wasn't even graphic," she said defensively. "And God only knows how you manage to help with branding, with that stomach."

"I ate something that didn't agree with me," he said icily.

"In that case, you must not have a lot of friends...."

The clerk doubled over laughing.

"I do not eat people!" Harley muttered.

"I should hope not," she replied. "I mean, being a cannibal is much worse than being a gardener."

"I am not a gardener!"

Alice gave the clerk a sweet smile. "Do you have chalk and colored string?" she asked. "I also need double-A batteries for my digital camera and some anti-bacterial hand cleaner."

The clerk looked blank.

Harley grinned. He knew this clerk very well. Sadly, Alice didn't. "Hey, John, this is a real, honest-to-goodness crime scene investigator," he told the young man. "She works out of the medical examiner's office in San Antonio!"

Alice felt her stomach drop as she noted the bright fascination in the clerk's eyes. The clerk's whole face became animated. "You do, really? Hey, I watch all those CSI shows," he exclaimed. "I know about DNA profiles. I even know how to tell how long a body's been dead just by identifying the insects on it...!"

"You have a great day, Ms. Jones," Harley told Alice, over the clerk's exuberant monologue.

She glared at him. "Oh, thanks very much."

He tipped his bibbed cap at her. "See you, John," he told the clerk. Harley picked up his purchases, smiling with pure delight, and headed right out the front door.

The clerk waved an absent hand in his general direction, never taking his eyes off Alice. "Anyway, about those insects," he began enthusiastically.

Alice followed him around the store for her supplies, groaning inwardly as he kept talking. She never ran out of people who could tell her how to do her job these days, thanks to the proliferation of television shows on forensics. She tried to explain that most labs were understaffed, under-budgeted, and that lab results didn't come back in an hour, even for a department like hers, on the University of Texas campus, which had a national reputation for excellence. But the bug expert here was on a roll and he wasn't listening. She resigned herself to the lecture and forced a smile. Wouldn't do to make enemies here, not when she might be doing more business with him later. She was going to get even with that smug cowboy the next time she saw him, though.

The riverbank was spitting out law enforcement people. Alice groaned as she bent to the poor body and began to take measurements. She'd already had an accommodating young officer from the Jacobsville Police Department run yellow police tape all around the crime scene. That didn't stop people from stepping over it, however.

"You stop that," Alice muttered at two men wearing deputy sheriff uniforms. They both stopped with one foot in the air at the tone of her voice. "No tramping around on my crime scene! That yellow tape is to keep people *out*."

"Sorry," one murmured sheepishly, and they both went back on their side of the line. Alice pushed away a strand of sweaty hair with the back of a latex-gloved hand and muttered to herself. It was almost Christmas, but the weather had gone nuts and it was hot. She'd already taken off her wool jacket and replaced it with a lab coat, but her slacks were wool and she was burning up. Not to mention that this guy had been lying on the riverbank for at least a day and he was ripe. She had Vicks Salve under her nose, but it wasn't helping a lot.

For the hundredth time, she wondered why she'd ever chosen such a messy profession. But it was very satisfying when she could help catch a murderer, which she had many times over the years. Not that it substituted for a family. But most men she met were repelled by her profession. Sometimes she tried to keep it to herself. But inevitably there would be a movie or a TV show that would mention some forensic detail and Alice would hold forth on the misinformation she noted. Sometimes it was rather graphic, like with the vengeful cowboy in the hardware store.

Then there would be the forced smiles. The excuses. And so it went. Usually that happened before the end of the first date. Or at least the second.

"I'll bet I'm the only twenty-six-year-old virgin in the whole damned state of Texas," she muttered to herself.

"Excuse me?" one of the deputies, a woman, exclaimed with wide, shocked eyes.

"That's right, you just look at me as if I sprouted horns and a tail," she murmured as she worked. "I know I'm an anachronism."

"That's not what I meant," the deputy said, chuckling. "Listen, there are a lot of women our ages with that attitude. I don't want some unspeakable condition that I catch from a man who passes himself around like a dish of peanuts at a bar. And do you think they're going to tell you they've got something?"

Alice beamed. "I like you."

She chuckled. "Thanks. I think of it as being sensible." She lowered her voice. "See Kilraven over there?" she asked, drawing Alice's eyes to the arrival of another local cop—even if he really was a fed pretending to be one. "They say his brother, Jon Blackhawk, has never had a woman in his life. And we think we're prudes!"

Alice chuckled. "That's what I heard, too. Sensible man!"

"Very." The deputy was picking up every piece of paper, every cigarette butt she could find with latex gloves on, bagging them for Alice for evidence. "What about that old rag, Jones, think I should put it in a bag, too? Look at this little rusty spot."

Alice glanced at it, frowning. It was old, but there was a trace of something on it, something newer than the rag. "Yes," she said. "I think it's been here for a while, but that's new trace evidence on it. Careful not to touch the rusty-looking spot."

"Blood, isn't it?" She nodded.

"You're good," Alice said.

"I came down from Dallas PD," she said. "I got tired of big-city crime. Things are a little less hectic here. In fact, this is my first DB since I joined Sheriff Carson's department."

"That's a real change, I know," Alice said. "I work

out of San Antonio. Not the quietest place in the world, especially on weekends."

Kilraven had walked right over the police tape and came up near the body.

"What do you think you're doing?" Alice exclaimed. "Kilraven...!"

"Look," he said, his keen silver eyes on the grass just under the dead man's right hand, which was clenched and depressed into the mud. "There's something white."

Alice followed his gaze. She didn't even see it at first. She'd moved so that it was in shadow. But when she shifted, the sunlight caught it. Paper. A tiny sliver of paper, just peeping out from under the dead man's thumb. She reached down with her gloved hand and brushed away the grass. There was a deep indentation in the soft, mushy soil, next to his hand; maybe a footprint. "I need my camera before I move it," she said, holding out her hand. The deputy retrieved the big digital camera from its bag and handed it to Alice, who documented the find and recorded it on a graph of the crime scene. Then, returning the camera, she slid a pencil gently under the hand, moving it until she was able to see the paper. She reached into her kit for a pair of tweezers and tugged it carefully from his grasp.

"It's a tiny, folded piece of paper," she said, frowning. "And thank God it hasn't rained."

"Amen," Kilraven agreed, peering at the paper in her hand.

"Good eyes," she added with a grin.

He grinned back. "Lakota blood." He chuckled. "Tracking is in my genes. My great-great-grandfather was at Little Big Horn."

"I won't ask on which side," she said in a loud whisper.

"No need to be coy. He rode with Crazy Horse's band."

"Hey, I read about that," the deputy said. "Custer's guys were routed, they say."

"One of the Cheyenne people said later that a white officer was killed down at the river in the first charge," he said. "He said the officer was carried up to the last stand by his men, and after that the soldiers seemed to lose heart and didn't fight so hard. They found Custer's brother, Tom, and a couple of ranking officers from other units, including Custer's brother-in-law, with Custer. It could indicate that the chain of command changed several times. Makes sense, if you think about it. If there was a charge, Custer would have led it. Several historians think that Custer's unit made it into the river before the Cheyenne came flying into it after them. If Custer was killed early, he'd have been carried up to the last stand ridge—an enlisted guy, they'd have left there in the river."

"I never read that Custer got killed early in the fight," the deputy exclaimed.

"I've only ever seen the theory in one book—a warrior was interviewed who was on the Indian side of the fight, and he said he thought Custer was killed in the first charge," he mused. "The Indians' side of the story didn't get much attention until recent years. They said there were no surviving eyewitnesses. Bull! There were several tribes of eyewitnesses. It was just that nobody thought their stories were worth hearing just after the battle. Not the massacre," he added before the deputy could speak. "Massacres are when you kill unarmed people. Custer's men all had guns."

The deputy grinned. "Ever think of teaching history?"

"Teaching's too dangerous a profession. That's why I joined the police force instead." Kilraven chuckled.

"Great news for law enforcement," Alice said. "You have good eyes."

"You'd have seen it for yourself, Jones, eventually," he replied. "You're the best."

"Wow! Did you hear that? Take notes," Alice told the deputy. "The next time I get yelled at for not doing my job right, I'm quoting Kilraven."

"Would it help?" he asked.

She laughed. "They're still scared of you up in San Antonio," she said. "One of the old patrolmen, Jacobs, turns white when they mention your name. I understand the two of you had a little dustup?"

"I threw him into a fruit display at the local supermarket. Messy business. Did you know that blackberries leave purple stains on skin?" he added conversationally.

"I'm a forensic specialist," Alice reminded him. "Can I ask why you threw him into a fruit display?"

"We were working a robbery and he started making these remarks about fruit with one of the gay officers standing right beside me. The officer in question couldn't do anything without getting in trouble." He grinned. "Amazing, how attitudes change with a little gentle adjustment."

"Hey, Kilraven, what are you doing walking around on the crime scene?" Cash Grier called from the sidelines.

"Don't fuss at him," Alice called back. "He just spotted a crucial piece of evidence. You should give him an award!"

There were catcalls from all the officers present.

"I should get an award!" he muttered as he went to join his boss. "I never take days off or vacations!"

"That's because you don't have a social life, Kilraven," one of the officers joked.

Alice stood up, staring at the local law enforcement uniforms surrounding the crime scene tape. She recognized at least two cars from other jurisdictions. There was even a federal car out there! It wasn't unusual in a sleepy county like Jacobs for all officers who weren't busy to congregate around an event like this. It wasn't every day that you found a murder victim in your area. But a federal car for a local murder?

As she watched, Garon Grier and Jon Blackhawk of the San Antonio district FBI office climbed out of the BuCar—the FBI's term for a bureau car—and walked over the tape to join Alice.

"What have you found?" Grier asked.

She pursed her lips, glancing from the assistant director of the regional FBI office, Grier, to Special Agent Jon Blackhawk. What a contrast! Grier was blond and Blackhawk had long, jet-black hair tied in a ponytail. They were both tall and well-built without being flashy about it. Garon Grier, like his brother Cash, was married. Jon Blackhawk was unattached and available. Alice wished she was his type. He was every bit as good-looking as his half brother Kilraven.

"I found some bits and pieces of evidence, with the deputy's help. Your brother," she told Jon, "found this." She held up the piece of paper in an evidence bag. "Don't touch," she cautioned as both men peered in. "I'm not unfolding it until I can get it into my lab. I won't risk losing any trace evidence out here."

Blackhawk pulled out a pad and started taking notes. "Where was it?" he asked.

"Gripped in the dead man's fingers, out of sight. Why are you here?" she asked. "This is a local matter."

Blackhawk was cautious. "Not entirely," he said.

Kilraven joined them. He and Blackhawk exchanged uneasy glances.

"Okay. Something's going on that I can't be told about. It's okay." She held up a hand. "I'm used to being a mushroom. Kept in the dark and fed with…"

"Never mind," Garon told her. He softened it with a smile. "We've had a tip. Nothing substantial. Just something that interests us about this case."

"And you can't tell me what the tip was?"

"We found a car in the river, farther down," Cash said quietly. "San Antonio plates."

"Maybe his?" Alice indicated the body.

"Maybe. We're running the plates now," Cash said.

"So, do you think he came down here on his own, or did somebody bring him in a trunk?" Alice mused.

The men chuckled. "You're good, Alice," Garon murmured.

"Of course I am!" she agreed. "Could you," she called to the female deputy, "get me some plaster of Paris out of my van, in the back? This may be a footprint where we found the piece of paper! Thanks."

She went back to work with a vengeance while two sets of brothers looked on with intent interest.

Two

Alice fell into her bed at the local Jacobsville motel after a satisfying soak in the luxurious whirlpool bathtub. Amazing, she thought, to find such a high-ticket item in a motel in a small Texas town. She was told that film crews from Hollywood frequently chose Jacobs County as a location and that the owner of the motel wanted to keep them happy. It was certainly great news for Alice.

She'd never been so tired. The crime scene, they found, extended for a quarter of a mile down the river. The victim had fought for his life. There were scuff marks and blood trails all over the place. So much for her theory that he'd traveled to Jacobsville in the trunk of the car they'd found.

The question was, why had somebody brought a man down to Jacobsville to kill him? It made no sense.

She closed her eyes, trying to put herself in the shoes of the murderer. People usually killed for a handful of reasons. They killed deliberately out of jealousy, anger or greed. Sometimes they killed accidentally. Often, it was an impulse that led to a death, or a series of acts that pushed a person over the edge. All too often, it was drugs or alcohol that robbed someone of impulse control, and that led inexorably to murder.

Few people went into an argument or a fight intending to kill someone. But it wasn't as if you could take it back even seconds after a human life expired. There were thousands of young people in prison who would have given anything to relive a single incident where they'd made a bad choice. Families suffered for those choices, along with their children. So often, it was easy to overlook the fact that even murderers had families, often decent, law-abiding families that agonized over what their loved one had done and paid the price along with them.

Alice rolled over, restlessly. Her job haunted her from time to time. Along with the coroner, and the investigating officers, she was the last voice of the deceased. She spoke for them, by gathering enough evidence to bring the killer to trial. It was a holy grail. She took her duties seriously. But she also had to live with the results of the murderer's lack of control. It was never pleasant to see a dead body. Some were in far worse conditions than others. She carried those memories as certainly as the family of the deceased carried them.

Early on, she'd learned that she couldn't let herself become emotionally involved with the victims. If she started crying, she'd never stop, and she wouldn't be effective in her line of work.

She found a happy medium in being the life of the

party at crime scenes. It diverted her from the misery of her surroundings and, on occasion, helped the crime scene detectives cope as well. One reporter, a rookie, had given her a hard time because of her attitude. She'd invited him to her office for a close-up look at the world of a real forensic investigator.

The reporter had arrived expecting the corpse, always tastefully displayed, to be situated in the tidy, high-tech surroundings that television crime shows had accustomed him to seeing.

Instead, Alice pulled the sheet from a drowning victim who'd been in the water three days.

She never saw the reporter again. Local cops who recounted the story, always with choked-back laughter, told her that he'd turned in his camera the same day and voiced an ambition to go into real estate.

Just as well, she thought. The real thing was pretty unpleasant. Television didn't give you the true picture, because there was no such thing as smell-o-vision. She could recall times when she'd gone through a whole jar of Vicks Salve trying to work on a drowning victim like the one she'd shown the critical member of the Fourth Estate.

She rolled over again. She couldn't get her mind to shut down long enough to allow for sleep. She was reviewing the meager facts she'd uncovered at the crime scene, trying to make some sort of sense out of it. Why would somebody drive a murder victim out of the city to kill him? Maybe because he didn't know he was going to become a murder victim. Maybe he got in the car voluntarily.

Good point, she thought. But it didn't explain the crime. Heat of passion wouldn't cover this one. It was too deliberate. The perp meant to hide evidence. And he had.

She sighed. She wished she'd become a detective instead of a forensic specialist. It must be more fun solving crimes than being knee-deep in bodies. And prospective dates wouldn't look at you from a safe distance with that expression of utter distaste, like that gardener in the hardware store this afternoon.

What had Grier called him, Fowler? Harley Fowler, that was it. Not a bad-looking man. He had a familiar face. Alice wondered why. She was sure she'd never seen him before today. She was sure she'd remember somebody that disagreeable.

Maybe he resembled somebody she knew. That was possible. Fowler. Fowler. No. It didn't ring any bells. She'd have to let her mind brood on it for a couple of days. Sometimes that's all it took to solve such puzzles—background working of the subconscious. She chuckled to herself. *Background workings,* she thought, *will save me yet.*

After hours of almost-sleep, she got up, dressed and went back to the crime scene. It was quiet, now, without the presence of almost every uniformed officer in the county. The body was lying in the local funeral home, waiting for transport to the medical examiner's office in San Antonio. Alice had driven her evidence up to San Antonio, to the crime lab, and turned it over to the trace evidence people, specifically Longfellow.

She'd entrusted Longfellow with the precious piece of paper which might yield dramatic evidence, once unfolded. There had clearly been writing on it. The dead man had grasped it tight in his hand while he was being killed, and had managed to conceal it from his killer. It must have something on it that he was desperate to preserve. Amazing. She wanted to know what it was. Tomorrow, she promised herself, their best trace evidence specialist, Longfellow, would have that paper turned every which way but loose in her lab, and she'd find answers for Alice. She was one of the best CSI people Alice had ever worked with. When Alice drove right back down to Jacobsville, she knew she'd have answers from the lab soon.

Restless, she looked around at the lonely landscape, bare in winter. The local police were canvassing the surrounding area for anyone who'd seen something unusual in the past few days, or who'd noticed an out-of-town car around the river.

Alice paced the riverbank, a lonely figure in a neat white sweatshirt with blue jeans, staring out across the ripples of the water while her sneakers tried to sink into the damp sand. It was cooler today, in the fifties, about normal for a December day in south Texas.

Sometimes she could think better when she was alone at the crime scene. Today wasn't one of those days. She was acutely aware of her aloneness. It was worse now, after the death of her father a month ago. He was her last living relative. He'd been a banker back in Tennessee, where she'd taken courses in forensics. The family was from Floresville, just down the road from San Antonio. But her parents had moved away to Tennessee when she was in her last year of high school, and that had been a wrench. Alice had a crush on a boy in her class, but the move killed any hope of a relationship. She really had been a late bloomer, preferring to hang out in the biology lab rather than think about dating. Amoeba under the microscope were so much more interesting.

Alice had left home soon after her mother's death, the year she started college. Her mother had been a live wire, a happy and well-adjusted woman who could do almost anything around the house, especially cook. She despaired of Alice, her only child, who watched endless reruns of the old TV show *Quincy,* about a medical examiner, along with archaic *Perry Mason* episodes. Long before it was popular, Alice had dreamed of being a crime scene technician.

She'd been an ace at biology in high school. Her science teachers had encouraged her, delighting in her bright enthusiasm. One of them had recommended her to a colleague at the University of Texas campus in San Antonio, who'd steered her into a science major and helped her find local scholarships to supplement the small amount her father could afford for her. It had been an uphill climb to get that degree, and to add to it with courses from far-flung universities when time and money permitted; one being courses in forensic anthropology at the University of Tennessee in Knoxville. In between, she'd slogged away with other techs at one crime scene after another, gaining experience.

Once, in her haste to finish gathering evidence, due to a rare prospective date, she'd slipped up and mislabeled blood evidence. That had cost the prosecution staff a conviction. It had been a sobering experience for Alice, especially when the suspect went out and killed a young boy before being rearrested. Alice felt responsible for that boy's death. She never forgot how haste had put the nails in his coffin, and she never slipped up again. She gained a reputation for being precise and meticulous in evidence-gathering. And she never went home early again. Alice was almost always the last person to leave the lab, or the crime scene, at the end of the day.

A revved-up engine caught her attention. She turned as a carload of young boys pulled up beside her white van at the river's edge.

"Lookie there, a lonely lady!" one of them called. "Ain't she purty?"

"Shore is! Hey, pretty thing, you like younger men? We can make you happy!"

"You bet!" Another one laughed.

"Hey, lady, you feel like a party?!" another one cat-called.

Alice glared. "No, I don't feel like a party. Take a hike!" She turned back to her contemplation of the river, hoping they'd give up and leave.

"Aww, that ain't no way to treat prospective boy-friends!" one yelled back. "Come on up here and lie down, lady. We want to talk to you!"

More raucous laughter echoed out of the car.

So much for patience. She was in no mood for teenagers acting out. She pulled out the pad and pen she always carried in her back pocket and walked up the bank and around to the back of their car. She wrote down the license plate number without being obvious about it. She'd call in a harassment call and let local law enforcement help her out. But even as she thought about it, she hesitated. There had to be a better way to handle this bunch of loonies without involving the law. She was overreacting. They were just teenagers, after all. Inspiration struck as she reemerged at the driver's side of the car.

She ruffled her hair and moved closer to the tow-headed young driver. She leaned down. "I like your tires," she drawled with a wide grin. "They're real nice. And wide. And they have treads. I *like* treads." She wiggled her eyebrows at him. "You like treads?"

He stared at her. The silly expression went into eclipse. "Treads?" His voice sounded squeaky. He tried again. "Tire…treads?"

"Yeah. Tire treads." She stuck her tongue in and out and grinned again. "I *reeaaally* like tire treads."

He was trying to pretend that he wasn't talking to a lunatic. "Uh. You do. Really."

She was enjoying herself now. The other boys seemed even more confused than the driver did. They were all staring at her. Nobody was laughing.

She frowned. "No, you don't like treads. You're just humoring me. Okay. If you don't like treads, you might like what I got in the truck," she said, lowering her voice. She jerked her head toward the van.

He cleared his throat. "I might like what you got in the truck," he parroted.

She nodded, grinning, widening her eyes until the whites almost gleamed. She leaned forward. "I got bodies in there!" she said in a stage whisper and levered her eyes wide-open. "Real dead bodies! Want to see?"

The driver gaped at her. Then he exclaimed, "Dead… bod…. Oh, Good Lord, no!"

He jerked back from her, slammed his foot down on the accelerator, and spun sand like dust as he roared back out onto the asphalt and left a rubber trail behind him.

She shook her head. "Was it something I said?" she asked a nearby bush.

She burst out laughing. She really did need a vacation, she told herself.

* * *

Harley Fowler saw the van sitting on the side of the road as he moved a handful of steers from one pasture to another. With the help of Bob, Cy Parks's veteran cattle dog, he put the little steers into their new area and closed the gate behind him. A carload of boys roared up beside the van and got noisy. They were obviously hassling the crime scene woman. Harley recognized her van.

His pale blue eyes narrowed and began to glitter. He didn't like a gang of boys trying to intimidate a lone woman. He reached into his saddlebag and pulled out his gunbelt, stepping down out of the saddle to strap it on. He tied the horse to a bar of the gate and motioned Bob to stay. Harley strolled off toward the van.

He didn't think he'd have to use the pistol, of course. The threat of it would be more than enough. But if any of the boys decided to have a go at him, he could put them down with his fists. He'd learned a lot from Eb Scott and the local mercs. He didn't need a gun to enforce his authority. But if the sight of it made the gang of boys a little more likely to leave without trouble, that was all right, too.

He moved into sight just at the back of Alice's van. She was leaning over the driver's side of the car. He couldn't hear what she said, but he could certainly hear what the boy exclaimed as he roared out onto the highway and took off.

Alice was talking to a bush.

Harley stared at her with confusion.

Alice sensed that she was no longer alone, and she turned. She blinked. "Have you been there long?" she asked hesitantly.

"Just long enough to see the Happy Teenager Gang

take a powder," he replied. "Oh, and to hear you asking a bush about why they left." His eyes twinkled. "Talk to bushes a lot in your line of work, do you?"

She was studying him curiously, especially the low-slung pistol in its holster. "You on your way to a gunfight and just stopped by to say hello?"

"I was moving steers," he replied. "I heard the teen-agers giving you a hard time and came to see if you needed any help. Obviously not."

"Were you going to offer to shoot them for me?" she asked.

He chuckled. "Never had to shoot any kids," he said with emphasis.

"You've shot other sorts of people?"

"One or two," he said pleasantly, but this time he didn't smile.

She felt chills go down her spine. If her livelihood made him queasy, the way he looked wearing that sidearm made her feel the same way. He wasn't the easygoing cowboy she'd met in town the day before. He reminded her oddly of Cash Grier, for reasons she couldn't put into words. There was cold steel in this man. He had the self-confidence of a man who'd been tested under fire. It was unusual, in a modern man. Unless, she considered, he'd been in the military, or some paramilitary unit.

"I don't shoot women," he said when she hesitated.

"Good thing," she replied absently. "I don't have any bandages."

He moved closer. She seemed shaken. He scowled. "You okay?"

She shifted uneasily. "I guess so."

"Mind telling me how you got them to leave so quickly?"

"Oh. That. I just asked if they'd like to see the dead bodies in my van."

He blinked. He was sure he hadn't heard her right. "You asked if…?" he prompted.

She sighed. "I guess it was a little over the top. I was going to call Hayes Carson and have him come out and save me, but it seemed a bit much for a little catcalling."

He didn't smile. "Let me tell you something. A little catcalling, if they get away with it, can lead to a little harassment, and if they get away with that, it can lead to a little assault, even if drugs or alcohol aren't involved. Boys need limits, especially at that age. You should have called it in and let Hayes Carson come out here and scare the hell out of them."

"Well, aren't you the voice of experience!"

"I should be," he replied. "When I was sixteen, an older boy hassled a girl in our class repeatedly on campus after school and made fun of me when I objected to it. A few weeks later, after she'd tried and failed to get somebody to do something about him, he assaulted her."

She let out a whistle. "Heavy stuff."

"Yes, and the teacher who thought I was overreacting when I told him was later disciplined for his lack of response," he added coldly.

"We live in difficult times," she said.

"Count on it."

She glanced in the direction the car had gone. "I still have the license plate number," she murmured.

"Give it to Hayes and tell him what happened," he encouraged her. "Even if you don't press charges, he'll keep an eye on them. Just in case."

She studied his face. "You liked that girl."

"Yes. She was sweet and kind-natured. She…"

She moved a little closer. "She…?"

"She killed herself," he said tightly. "She was very religious. She couldn't live with what happened, especially after she had to testify to it in court and everyone knew."

"They seal those files…" she began.

"Get real," he shot back. "It happened in a small town just outside San Antonio, not much bigger than Jacobsville. I was living there temporarily with a nice older couple and going to school with her when it happened. The people who sat on the jury and in the courtroom were all local. They knew her."

"Oh," she said softly. "I'm sorry."

He nodded.

"How long did the boy get?"

"He was a juvenile," he said heavily. "He was under eighteen when it happened. He stayed in detention until he was twenty-one and they turned him loose."

"Pity."

"Yes." He shook himself as if the memory had taken him over and he wanted to be free of it. "I never heard anything about him after that. I hope he didn't prosper."

"Was he sorry, do you think?"

He laughed coldly. "Sorry he got caught, yes."

"I've seen that sort in court," she replied, her eyes darkening with the memory. "Cocky and self-centered, contemptuous of everybody around them. Especially people in power."

"Power corrupts," he began.

"And absolute power corrupts absolutely," she finished for him. "Lord Acton," she cited belatedly.

"Smart gent." He nodded toward the river. "Any new thoughts on the crime scene?"

She shook her head. "I like to go there alone and

think. Sometimes I get ideas. I still can't figure how he died here, when he was from San Antonio, unless he came voluntarily with someone and didn't know they were going to kill him when they arrived."

"Or he came down here to see somebody," he returned, "and was ambushed."

"Wow," she said softly, turning to face him. "You're good."

There was a faint, ruddy color on his high cheekbones. "Thanks."

"No, I mean it," she said when she saw his expression. "That wasn't sarcasm."

He relaxed a little.

"We got off to a bad start, and it's my fault," Alice admitted. "Dead bodies make me nervous. I'm okay once I get started documenting things. It's the first sight of it that upsets me. You caught me at a bad time, at the hardware store. I didn't mean to embarrass you."

"Nothing embarrasses me," he said easily.

"I'm sorry, just the same."

He relaxed a little more.

She frowned as she studied his handsome face. He really was good-looking. "You look so familiar to me," she said. "I can't understand why. I've never met you before."

"They say we all have a doppelgänger," he mused. "Someone who looks just like us."

"Maybe that's it," she agreed. "San Antonio is a big city, for all its small-town atmosphere. We've got a lot of people. You must resemble someone I've seen."

"Probably."

She looked again at the crime scene. "I hope I can get enough evidence to help convict somebody of this. It was a really brutal murder. I don't like to think of people who can do things like that being loose in society."

He was watching her, adding up her nice figure and her odd personality. She was unique. He liked her. He wasn't admitting it, of course.

"How did you get into forensic work?" he asked. "Was it all those crime shows on TV?"

"It was the *Quincy* series," she confessed. "I watched reruns of it on TV when I was a kid. It fascinated me. I liked him, too, but it was the work that caught my attention. He was such an advocate for the victims." Her eyes became soft with reminiscence. "I remember when evidence I collected solved a crime. It was my first real case. The parents of the victim came over and hugged me after the prosecutor pointed me out to them. I always went to the sentencing if I could get away, in cases I worked. That was the first time I realized how important my work was." She grinned wickedly. "The convicted gave me the finger on his way out of the courtroom with a sheriff's deputy. I grinned at him. Felt good. Really good."

He laughed. It was a new sound, and she liked it.

"Does that make me less spooky?" she asked, moving a step closer.

"Yes, it does."

"You think I'm, you know, normal?"

"Nobody's really normal. But I know what you mean," he said, and he smiled at her, a genuine smile. "Yes, I think you're okay."

She cocked her head up at him and her blue eyes twinkled. "Would you believe that extraordinarily handsome Hollywood movie stars actually call me up for dates?"

"Do they, really?" he drawled.

"No, but doesn't it sound exciting?"

He laughed again.

She moved another step closer. "What I said, about not purchasing you if you were on sale in a groom shop…I didn't really mean it. There's a nice ring in that jewelry shop in Jacobsville," she said dreamily. "A man's wedding ring." She peered up through her lashes. "I could buy it for you."

He pursed his lips. "You could?"

"Yes. And I noticed that there's a minister at that Methodist Church. Are you Methodist?"

"Not really."

"Neither am I. Well, there's a justice of the peace in the courthouse. She marries people."

He was just listening now. His eyes were wide.

"If you liked the ring, and if it fit, we could talk to the justice of the peace. They also have licenses."

He pursed his lips again. "Whoa," he said after a minute. "I only met you yesterday."

"I know." She blinked. "What does that have to do with getting married?"

"I don't know you."

"Oh. Okay. I'm twenty-six. I still have most of my own teeth." She displayed them. "I'm healthy and athletic, I like to knit but I can hunt, too, and I have guns. I don't like spinach, but I love liver and onions. Oh, and I'm a virgin." She smiled broadly.

He was breathless by this time. He stared at her intently.

"It's true," she added when he didn't comment. She scowled. "Well, I don't like diseases and you can't look at a man and tell if he has one." She hesitated. Frowned worriedly. "You don't have any…?"

"No, I don't have any diseases," he said shortly. "I'm fastidious about women."

"What a relief!" she said with a huge sigh. "Well, that covers all the basics." Her blue eyes smiled up at him and she batted her long black eyelashes. "So when do we see the justice of the peace?"

"Not today," he replied. "I'm washing Bob."

"Bob?"

He pointed toward the cattle dog, who was still sitting at the pasture gate. He whistled. Bob came running up to him, wagging her long, silky tail and hassling. She looked as if she was always smiling.

"Hi, Bob," Alice said softly, and bent to offer a hand, which Bob smelled. Then Alice stroked the silky head. "Nice boy."

"Girl," he corrected. "Bob's a girl."

She blinked at him.

"Mr. Parks said if Johnny Cash could have a boy named Sue, he could have a girl dog named Bob."

"He's got a point," she agreed. She ruffled Bob's fur affectionately. "You're a beaut, Bob," she told the dog.

"She really is. Best cattle dog in the business, and she can get into places in the brush that we can't, on horseback, to flush out strays."

"Do you come from a ranching family?" she asked absently as she stroked the dog.

"Actually I didn't know much about cattle when I went to work for Mr. Parks. He had one of his men train me."

"Wow. Nice guy."

"He is. Dangerous, but nice."

She lifted her head at the use of the word and frowned slightly. "Dangerous?"

"Do you know anything about Eb Scott and his outfit?"

"The mercenary." She nodded. "We all know about his training camp down here. A couple of our officers use his firing range. He made it available to everyone in law enforcement. He's got friends in our department."

"Well, he and Mr. Parks and Dr. Micah Steele were part of a group who used to make their living as mercenaries."

"I remember now," she exclaimed. "There was a shoot-out with some of that drug lord Lopez's men a few years ago!"

"Yes. I was in it."

She let out a breath. "Brave man, to go up against those bozos. They carry automatic weapons."

"I noticed." That was said with a droll expression worth a hundred words.

She searched his eyes with quiet respect. "Now, I really want to see the justice of the peace. I'd be safe anywhere."

He laughed. "I'm not that easy. You haven't even brought me flowers, or asked me out to a nice restaurant."

"Oh, dear."

"What?"

"I don't get paid until Friday, and I'm broke," she said sorrowfully. She made a face. "Well, maybe next week? Or we could go dutch…"

He chuckled with pure delight. "I'm broke, too."

"So, next week?"

"We'll talk about it."

She grinned. "Okay."

"Better get your van going," he said, holding out a palm-up hand and looking up. "We're going to get a rain shower. You could be stuck in that soft sand when it gets wet."

"I could. See you."

"See you."

She took off running for the van. Life was looking up, she thought happily.

Three

Harley went back to the ranch house with Bob racing beside his horse. He felt exhilarated for the first time in years. Usually he got emotionally involved with girls who were already crazy about some other man. He was the comforting shoulder, the listening ear. But Alice Jones seemed to really like him.

Of course, there was her profession. He felt cold when he thought about her hands working on dead tissue. That was a barrier he'd have to find some way to get past. Maybe by concentrating on what a cute woman she was.

Cy Parks was outside, looking over a bunch of young bulls in the corral. He looked up when Harley dismounted.

"What do you think, Harley?" he asked, nodding toward several very trim young Santa Gertrudis bulls.

"Nice," he said. "These the ones you bought at the

auction we went to back in October? Gosh, they've grown!"

He nodded. "They are. I brought them in to show to J. D. Langley. He's looking for some young bulls for his own herd. I thought I'd sell him a couple of these. Good thing I didn't have to send them back."

Harley chuckled. "Good thing, for the seller. I remember the lot we sent back last year. I had to help you deliver them."

"Yes, I remember," Cy replied. "He slugged you and I slugged him."

Harley resisted a flush. It made him feel good, that Mr. Parks liked him enough to defend him. He could hardly recall his father. It had been years since they'd had any contact at all. He felt a little funny recalling how he'd lied to his boss about his family, claiming that his mother could help brand cattle and his father was a mechanic. He'd gone to live with an older couple he knew after a fight with his real folks. It was a small ranch they owned, but only the wife lived on it. Harley had stayed in town with the husband at his mechanic's shop most of the time. He hadn't been interested in cattle at the time. Now, they were his life and Mr. Parks had taken the place of his father, although Harley had never put it into words. Someday, he guessed, he was going to have to tell his boss the truth about himself. But not today.

"Have any trouble settling the steers in their new pasture?" Cy asked.

"None at all. The forensic lady was out at the river."

"Alice Jones?"

"Yes. She said sometimes she likes to look around crime scenes alone. She gets impressions." He smiled.

"I helped her with an idea about how the murder was committed."

Parks looked at him and smiled. "You've got a good brain, Harley."

He grinned. "Thanks."

"So what was your idea?"

"Maybe the victim was here to see somebody and got ambushed."

Parks's expression became solemn. "That's an interesting theory. If she doesn't share it with Hayes Carson, you should. There may be somebody local involved in all this."

"That's not a comforting thought."

"I know." He frowned as he noted the gun and holster Harley was wearing. "Did we have a gunfight and I wasn't invited?"

"This?" Harley fingered the butt of the gun. "Oh. No! There were some local boys trying to harass Alice. I strapped it on for effect and went to help her, but she'd already sent them running."

"Threatened to call the cops, huh?" he asked pleasantly.

"She invited them to her van to look at bodies," he said, chuckling. "They left tread marks on the highway."

He grinned back. "Well! Sounds like she has a handle on taking care of herself."

"Yes. But we all need a little backup, from time to time," Harley said.

Cy put a hand on Harley's shoulder. "You were mine, that night we had the shoot-out with the drug dealers. You're a good man under fire."

"Thanks," Harley said, flushing a little with the praise. "You'll never know how I felt, when you said that, after we got home."

"Maybe I do. See about that cattle truck, will you? I

think it's misfiring again, and you're the best mechanic we've got."

"I'll do it. Just don't tell Buddy you meant it," he pleaded. "He's supposed to be the mechanic."

"Supposed to be is right," Cy huffed. "But I guess you've got a point. Try to tell him, in a nice way, that he needs to check the spark plugs."

"You could tell him," Harley began.

"Not the way you can. If I tell him, he'll quit." He grimaced. "Already lost one mechanic that way this year. Can't afford to lose another. You do it."

Harley laughed. "Okay. I'll find a way."

"You always do. Don't know what I'd do without you, Harley. You're an asset as a foreman." He studied the younger man quietly. "I never asked where you came from. You said you knew cattle, but you really didn't. You learned by watching, until I hooked you up with old Cal and let him tutor you. I always respected the effort you put in, to learn the cattle business. But you're still as mysterious as you were the day you turned up."

"Sometimes it's better to look ahead, and not backward," Harley replied.

Parks smiled. "Enough said. See you later."

"Sure."

He walked off toward the house where his young wife, Lisa, was waiting with one preschool-aged boy and one infant boy in her arms. Of all the people Harley would never have expected to marry, Mr. Parks was first on his list. The rancher had been reclusive, hard to get along with and, frankly, bad company. Lisa had changed him. Now, it was impossible to think of him as anything except a family man. Marriage had mellowed him.

Harley thought about what Parks had said, about how mysterious he was. Maybe Mr. Parks thought he was running from the law. That was a real joke. Harley was running from his family. He'd had it up to his neck with monied circles and important people and parents who thought position was everything. They'd argued heatedly one summer several years ago, when Harley was sixteen, about Harley's place in the family and his lack of interest in their social life. He'd walked out.

He had a friend whose aunt and uncle owned a small ranch and had a mechanic's shop in Floresville. He'd taken Harley down there and they'd invited him to move in. He'd had his school files transferred to the nearest high school and he'd started his life over. His parents had objected, but they hadn't tried to force him to come back home. He graduated and went into the Army. But, just after he returned to Texas following his release from the Army, he went to see his parents and saw that nothing had changed at all. He was expected to do his part for the family by helping win friends and influencing the right people. Harley had left that very night, paid cash for a very old beat-up pickup truck and turned himself into a vagabond cowhand looking for work.

He'd gone by to see the elderly couple he'd lived with during his last year of high school, but the woman had died, the ranch had been sold and the mechanic had moved to Dallas. Discouraged, Harley had been driving through Jacobsville looking for a likely place to hire on when he'd seen cowboys working cattle beside the road. He'd talked to them and heard that Cy Parks was hiring. The rest was history.

He knew that people wondered about him. He kept his silence. It was new and pleasant to be accepted at face value, to have people look at him for who he was and what he knew how to do rather than at his background. He was happy in Jacobsville.

He did wonder sometimes if his people missed him. He read about them in the society columns. There had been a big political dustup just recently and a landslide victory for a friend of his father's. That had caught his attention. But it hadn't prompted him to try to mend fences. Years had passed since his sudden exodus from San Antonio, but it was still too soon for that. No, he liked being just plain Harley Fowler, cowboy. He wasn't risking his hard-won place in Jacobsville for anything.

Alice waited for Hayes Carson in his office, frowning as she looked around. Wanted posters. Reams of paperwork. A computer that was obsolete, paired with a printer that was even more obsolete. An old IBM Selectric typewriter. A battered metal wastebasket that looked as if it got kicked fairly often. A CB unit. She shook her head. There wasn't one photograph anywhere in the room, except for a framed one of Hayes's father, Dallas, who'd been sheriff before him. Nothing personal.

Hayes walked in, reading a sheet of paper.

"You really travel light, don't you?" Alice mused.

He looked up, surprised. "Why do you say that?"

"This is the most impersonal office I've ever walked into. Wait." She held up a hand. "I take that back. Jon Blackhawk's office is worse. He doesn't even have a photograph in his."

"My dad would haunt me if I removed his." He chuckled, sitting down behind the desk.

"Heard anything from the feds?"

"Yes. They got a report back on the car. It was reported missing by a woman who works for a San Antonio politician yesterday. She has no idea who took it."

"Damn." She sighed and leaned back. "Well, Longfellow's working on that piece of paper I found at the crime scene and we may get something from the cast I made of the footprint. We did find faint sole markings, from a sneaker. FBI lab has the cast. They'll track down which company made the shoe and try to trace where it was sold."

"That's a damned long shot."

"Hey, they've solved crimes from chips of paint."

"I guess so."

She was deep in thought. "Odd, how that paper was pushed into the dirt under his hand."

"Somebody stepped on it," Hayes reminded her.

"No." Her eyes narrowed. "It was clenched in the victim's hand and hidden under it."

Hayes frowned. "Maybe the victim was keeping it hidden deliberately?"

She nodded. "Like, maybe he knew he was going to die and wanted to leave a clue that might bring his killer to justice."

Hayes chuckled. "Jones, you watch too many crime dramas on TV."

"Actually, to hear the clerk at the hardware tell it I don't watch enough," she sighed. "I got a ten-minute lecture on forensic entomology while he hunted up some supplies I needed."

"Bug forensics?" he asked.

She nodded. "You can tell time of death by insect activity. I've actually taken courses on it. And I've solved at least one murder with the help of a bug expert." She pushed back a stray wisp of dark hair. "But what's really interesting, Carson, is teeth."

He frowned. "Teeth?"

She nodded. "Dentition. You can tell so much about a DB from its teeth, especially if there are dental records available. For example, there's Carabelli's cusp, which is most frequently found in people of European ancestry. Then there's the Uto-Aztecan upper premolar with a bulging buccal cusp which is found only in Native Americans. You can identify Asian ancestry in shovel-shaped incisors… Well, anyway, your ancestry, even the story of your life, is in your teeth. Your diet, your age…"

"Whether you got in bar fights," he interrupted.

She laughed. "Missing some teeth, are we?"

"Only a couple," he said easily. "I've calmed right down in my old age."

"You and Kilraven," she agreed dubiously.

He laughed. "Not that yahoo," he corrected. "Kilraven will never calm down, and you can quote me."

"He might, if he can ever slay his demons." She frowned thoughtfully and narrowed her eyes. "We have a lot of law enforcement down here that works in San Antonio." She was thinking out loud. "There's Garon Grier, the assistant SAC in the San Antonio field office. There's Rick Marquez, who works as a detective for San Antonio P.D. And then there's Kilraven."

"You trying to say something?" he asked.

She shook her head. "I'm linking unconnected facts. Sometimes it helps. Okay, here goes. A guy comes down here from San Antonio and gets whacked. He's driving somebody else's stolen car. He's messed up so badly that his own mother couldn't identify him. Whoever killed him didn't want him ID'd."

"Lots of reasons for that, maybe."

"Maybe. Hear me out. I'm doing pattern associations." She got up, locked her hands behind her waist, and started pacing, tossing out thoughts as they presented themselves. "Of all those law enforcement people, Kilraven's been the most conspicuous in San Antonio lately. He was with his brother, Jon, when they tried to solve the kidnapping of Gracie Marsh, Jason Pendleton's stepsister…"

"Pendleton's wife, now," he interrupted with a grin.

She returned it. "He was also connected with the rescue of Rodrigo Ramirez, the DEA agent kidnapping victim whose wife, Glory, was an assistant D.A. in San Antonio."

Hayes leaned back in his chair. "That wasn't made public, any of it."

She nodded absently.

"Rick Marquez has been pretty visible, too," he pointed out. He frowned. "Wasn't Rick trying to convince Kilraven to let him reopen that murder case that involved his family?"

"Come to think of it, yes," she replied, stopping in front of the desk. "Kilraven refused. He said it would only resurrect all the pain, and the media would dine out on it. He and Jon both refused. They figured it was a random crime and the perp was long gone."

"But that wasn't the end of it."

"No," she said. "Marquez refused to quit. He promised to do his work on the QT and not reveal a word of it to anybody except the detective he brought in to help him sort through the old files." She grimaced. "But the investigation went nowhere. Less than a week into their project, Marquez and his fellow detective were told to drop the investigation."

Hayes pursed his lips. "Now isn't that interesting?"

"There's more," she said. "Marquez and the detective went to the D.A. and promised to get enough evidence to reopen the case if they were allowed to continue. The D.A. said to let him talk to a few people. The very next week, the detective who was working with Marquez on the case was suddenly pulled off Homicide and sent back to the uniformed division as a patrol sergeant. And Marquez was told politely to keep his nose out of the matter and not to pursue it any further."

Hayes was frowning now. "You know, it sounds very much as if somebody high up doesn't want that case reopened. And I have to ask why?"

She nodded. "Somebody is afraid the case may be solved. If I'm guessing right, somebody with an enormous amount of power in government."

"And we both know what happens when power is abused," Hayes said with a scowl. "Years ago, when I was still a deputy sheriff, one of my fellow deputies—a new recruit—decided on his own to investigate rumors of a house of prostitution being run out of a local motel. Like a lamb, he went to the county council and brought it up in an open meeting."

Alice grimaced, because she knew from long experience what most likely happened after that. "Poor guy!"

"Well, after he was fired and run out of town," Hayes said, "I was called in and told that I was not to involve myself in that case, if I wanted to continue as a deputy sheriff in this county. I'd made the comment that no law officer should be fired for doing his job, you see."

"What did you do?" she asked, because she knew Hayes. He wasn't the sort of person to take a threat like that lying down.

"Ran for sheriff and won," he said simply. He grinned. "Turns out the head of the county council was getting kickbacks from the pimp. I found out, got the evidence and called a reporter I knew in San Antonio."

"That reporter?" she exclaimed. "He got a Pulitzer Prize for the story! My gosh, Hayes, the head of the county council went to prison! But it was for more than corruption…"

"He and the pimp also ran a modest drug distribution ring," he interrupted. "He'll be going up before the parole board in a few months. I plan to attend the hearing." He smiled. "I do so enjoy these little informal board meetings."

"Ouch."

"People who go through life making their money primarily through dishonest dealings don't usually reform," he said quietly. "It's a basic character trait that no amount of well-meaning rehabilitation can reverse."

"We live among some very unsavory people."

"Yes. That's why we have law enforcement. I might add, that the law enforcement on the county level here is exceptional."

She snarled at him. He just grinned.

"What's your next move?" she asked.

"I'm not making one until I know what's in that note. Shouldn't your assistant have something by now, even if it's only the text of the message?"

"She should." Alice pulled out her cell phone and called her office. "But I'm probably way off base about Kilraven's involvement in this. Maybe the victim just ticked off the wrong people and paid for it. Maybe he had unpaid drug bills or something."

"That's always a possibility," Hayes had to agree.

The phone rang and rang. Finally it was answered. "Crime lab, Longfellow speaking."

"Did you know that you have the surname of a famous poet?" Alice teased.

The other woman was all business, all the time, and she didn't get jokes. "Yes. I'm a far-removed distant cousin of the poet, in fact. You want to know about your scrap of paper, I suppose? It's much too early for any analysis of the paper or ink…"

"The writing, Longfellow, the writing," Alice interrupted.

"As I said, it's too early in the analysis. We'd need a sample to compare, first, and then we'd need a hand-writing expert…"

"But what does the message *say?*" Alice blurted out impatiently. Honest to God, the other woman was so ponderously slow sometimes!

"Oh, that. Just a minute." There was a pause, some paper ruffling, a cough. Longfellow came back on the line. "It doesn't say anything."

"You can't make out the letters? Is it waterlogged, or something?"

"It doesn't have letters."

"Then what does it have?" Alice said with the last of her patience straining at the leash. She was picturing Longfellow on the floor with herself standing over the lab tech with a large studded bat…

"It has numbers, Jones," came the droll reply. "Just a few numbers. Nothing else."

"An address?"

"Not likely."

"Give me the numbers."

"Only the last six are visible. The others apparently

were obliterated by the man's sweaty palms when he clenched it so tightly. Here goes."

She read the series of numbers.

"Which ones were obliterated?" Alice asked.

"Looks like the ones at the beginning. If it's a telephone number, the area code and the first of the exchange numbers is missing. We'll probably be able to reconstruct those at the FBI lab, but not immediately. Sorry."

"No, listen, you've been a world of help. If I controlled salaries, you'd get a raise."

"Why, thank you, Jones," came the astonished reply. "That's very kind of you to say."

"You're very welcome. Let me know if you come up with anything else."

"Of course I will."

Alice hung up. She looked at the numbers and frowned.

"What have you got?" Hayes asked.

"I'm not sure. A telephone number, perhaps."

He moved closer and peered at the paper where she'd written those numbers down. "Could that be the exchange?" he asked, noting some of the numbers.

"I don't know. If it is, it could be a San Antonio number, but we'd need to have the area code to determine that, and it's missing."

"Get that lab busy."

She glowered at him. "Like we sleep late, take two-hour coffee breaks, and wander into the crime lab about noon daily!"

"Sorry," he said, and grinned.

She pursed her full lips and gave him a roguish look. "Hey, you law enforcement guys live at doughnut shops and lounge around in the office reading sports magazines and playing games on the computer, right?"

He glowered back.

She held out one hand, palm up. "Welcome to the stereotype club."

"When will she have some more of those numbers?"

"Your guess is as good as mine. Has anybody spoken to the woman whose car was stolen to ask if someone she knew might have taken it? Or to pump her for information and find out if she really loaned it to him?" she added shrewdly.

"No, nobody's talked to her. The feds in charge of the investigation wanted to wait until they had enough information to coax her into giving them something they needed," he said.

"As we speak, they're roping Jon Blackhawk to his desk chair and gagging him," she pronounced with a grin. "His first reaction would be to drag her downtown and grill her."

"He's young and hotheaded. At least to hear his brother tell it."

"Kilraven loves his brother," Alice replied. "But he does know his failings."

"I wouldn't call rushing in headfirst a failing," Hayes pointed out.

"That's why you've been shot, Hayes," she said.

"Anybody can get shot," he said.

"Yes, but you've been shot twice," she reminded him. "The word locally is that you'd have a better chance of being named king of some small country than you'd have getting a wife. Nobody around here is rushing to line up and become a widow."

"I've calmed down," he muttered defensively. "And who's been saying that, anyway?"

"I heard that Minette Raynor was," she replied without quite meeting his eyes.

His jaw tautened. "I have no desire to marry Miss Raynor, now or ever," he returned coldly. "She helped kill my brother."

"She didn't, and you have proof, but suit yourself," she said when he looked angry enough to say something unforgivable. "Now, do you have any idea how we can talk to that woman before somebody shuts her up? It looks like whoever killed that poor man on the river wouldn't hesitate to give him company. I'd bet my reputation that he knew something that could bring down someone powerful, and he was stopped dead first. If the woman has any info at all, she's on the endangered list."

"Good point," Hayes had to admit. "Do you have a plan?"

She shook her head. "I wish."

"About that number, you might run it by the 911 operators," he said. "They deal with a lot of telephone traffic. They might recognize it."

"Now that's constructive thinking," she said with a grin. "But this isn't my jurisdiction, you know."

"The crime was committed in the county. That's my jurisdiction. I'm giving you the authority to investigate."

"Won't your own investigator feel slighted?"

"He would if he was here," he sighed. "He took his remaining days off and went to Wyoming for Christmas. He said he'd lose them if he didn't use them by the end of the year. I couldn't disagree and we didn't have much going on when I let him go." He shook his head. "He'll punch me when he gets back and discovers that we had a real DB right here and he didn't get to investigate it."

"The way things look," she said slowly, "he may still

get to help. I don't think we're going to solve this one in a couple of days."

"Hey, I saw a murder like this one on one of those CSI shows," he said with pretended excitement. "They sent trace evidence out, got results in two hours and had the guy arrested and convicted and sent to jail just before the last commercial!"

She gave him a smile and a gesture that was universal before she picked up her purse, and the slip of paper, and left his office.

She was eating lunch at Barbara's Café in town when the object of her most recent daydreams walked in, tall and handsome in real cowboy duds, complete with a shepherd's coat, polished black boots and a real black Stetson cowboy hat with a brim that looked just like the one worn by Richard Boone in the television series *Have Gun Will Travel* that she used to watch videos of. It was cocked over his eyes and he looked as much like a desperado as he did a working cowboy.

He spotted Alice as he was paying for his meal at the counter and grinned at her. She turned over a cup of coffee and it spilled all over the table, which made his grin much bigger.

Barbara came running with a towel. "Don't worry, it happens all the time," she reassured Alice. She glanced at Harley, put some figures together and chuckled. "Ah, romance is in the air."

"It is not," Alice said firmly. "I offered to take him to a movie, but I'm broke, and he won't go dutch treat," she added in a soft wail.

"Aww," Barbara sympathized.

"I don't get paid until next Friday," Alice said,

dabbing at wet spots on her once-immaculate oyster-white wool slacks. "I'll be miles away by then."

"I get paid this Friday," Harley said, straddling a chair opposite Alice with a huge steak and fries on a platter. "Are you having a salad for lunch?" he asked, aghast at the small bowl at her elbow. "You'll never be able to do any real investigating on a diet like that. You need protein." He indicated the juicy, rare steak on his own plate.

Alice groaned. He didn't understand. She'd spent so many hours working in her lab that she couldn't really eat a steak anymore. It was heresy here in Texas, so she tended to keep her opinions to herself. If she said anything like that, there would be a riot in Barbara's Café.

So she just smiled. "Fancy seeing you here," she teased.

He grinned. "I'll bet it wasn't a surprise," he said as he began to carve his steak.

"Whatever do you mean?" she asked with pretended innocence.

"I was just talking to Hayes Carson out on the street and he happened to mention that you asked him where I ate lunch," he replied.

She huffed. "Well, that's the last personal question I'll ever ask him, and you can take that to the bank!"

"Should I mention that I asked him where *you* ate lunch?" he added with a twinkle in his pale eyes.

Alice's irritated expression vanished. She sighed. "Did you, really?" she asked.

"I did, really. But don't take that as a marriage proposal," he said. "I almost never propose to crime scene investigators over lunch."

"Crime scene investigators?" a cowboy from one of the nearby ranches exclaimed, leaning toward them.

"Listen, I watch those shows all the time. Did you know that they can tell time of death by…!"

"Oh, dear, I'm so sorry!" Alice exclaimed as the cowboy gaped at her. She'd "accidentally" poured a glass of iced tea all over him. "It's a reflex," she tried to explain as Barbara came running, again. "You see, every time somebody talks about the work I do, I just get all excited and start throwing things!" She picked up her salad bowl. "It's a helpless reflex, I just can't stop…"

"No problem!" the cowboy said at once, scrambling to his feet. "I had to get back to work anyway! Don't think a thing about it!"

He rushed out the door, trailing tea and ice chips, leaving behind half a cup of coffee and a couple of bites of pie and an empty plate.

Harley was trying not to laugh, but he lost it completely. Barbara was chuckling as she motioned to one of her girls to get a broom and pail.

"I'm sorry," Alice told her. "Really."

Barbara gave her an amused glance. "You don't like to talk shop at the table, do you?"

"No. I don't," she confessed.

"Don't worry," Barbara said as the broom and pail and a couple of paper towels were handed to her. "I'll make sure word gets around. Before lunch tomorrow," she added, still laughing.

Four

After that, nobody tried to engage Alice in conversation about her job. The meal was pleasant and friendly. Alice liked Harley. He had a good personality, and he actually improved on closer acquaintance, as so many people didn't. He was modest and unassuming, and he didn't try to monopolize the conversation.

"How's your investigation coming?" he asked when they were on second cups of black coffee.

She shrugged. "Slowly," she replied. "We've got a partial number, possibly a telephone number, a stolen car whose owner didn't know it was stolen and a partial sneaker track that we're hoping someone can identify."

"I saw a program on the FBI lab that showed how they do that," Harley replied. He stopped immediately as soon as he realized what he'd said. He sat with his fork poised in midair, eyeing Alice's refilled coffee mug.

She laughed. "Not to worry. I'll control my reflexes. Actually the lab does a very good job running down sneaker treads," she added. "The problem is that most treads are pretty common. You get the name of a company that produces them and then start wearing out shoe leather going to stores and asking for information about people who bought them."

"What about people who paid cash and there's no record of their buying them?"

"I never said investigation techniques were perfect," she returned, smiling. "We use what we can get."

He frowned. "Those numbers, it shouldn't be that hard to isolate a telephone number, should it? You could narrow it down with a computer program."

"Yes, but there are so many possible combinations, considering that we don't even have the area code." She groaned. "And we'll have to try every single one."

He pursed his lips. "The car, then. Are you sure the person who owned it didn't have a connection to the murder victim?"

She raised her eyebrows. "Ever considered a career in law enforcement?"

He laughed. "I did, once. A long time ago." He grimaced, as if the memory wasn't a particularly pleasant one.

"We're curious about the car," she said, "but they don't want to spook the car's owner. It turns out that she works for a particularly unpleasant member of the political community."

His eyebrows lifted. "Who?"

She hesitated.

"Come on. I'm a clam. Ask my boss."

"Okay. It's the senior U.S. senator from Texas who lives in San Antonio," she confessed.

Harley made an ungraceful movement and sat back in his chair. He stared toward the window without really seeing anything. "You think the politician may be connected in some way?"

"There's no way of knowing right now," she sighed. "Everybody big in political circles has people who work for them. Anybody can get involved with a bad person and not know it."

"Are they going to question the car owner?"

"I'm sure they will, eventually. They just want to pick the right time to do it."

He toyed with his coffee cup. "So, are you staying here for a while?"

She grimaced. "A few more days, just to see if I can develop any more leads. Hayes Carson wants me to look at the car while the lab's processing it, so I guess I'll go up to San Antonio for that and come back here when I'm done."

He just nodded, seemingly distracted.

She studied him with a whimsical expression. "So, when are we getting married?" she asked.

He gave her an amused look. "Not today. I have to move cattle."

"My schedule is very flexible," she assured him.

He smiled. "Mine isn't."

"Rats."

"Now, that's interesting, I was just thinking about rats. I have to get cat food while I'm in town."

She blinked. "Cat food. For rats?"

"We keep barn cats to deal with the rat problem," he

explained. "But there aren't quite enough mice and rats to keep the cats healthy, so we supplement."

"I like cats," she said with a sigh and a smile. "Maybe we could adopt some stray ones when we get married." She frowned. "Now that's going to be a problem."

"Cats are?"

"No. Where are we going to live?" she persisted. "My job is in San Antonio and yours is here. I know," she said, brightening. "I'll commute!"

He laughed. She made him feel light inside. He finished his coffee. "Better work on getting the bridegroom first," he pointed out.

"Okay. What sort of flowers do you like, and when are we going on our first date?"

He pursed his lips. She was outrageously forward, but behind that bluff personality, he saw something deeper and far more fragile. She was shy. She was like a storefront with piñatas and confetti that sold elegant silverware. She was disguising her real persona with an exaggerated one.

He leaned back in his chair, feeling oddly arrogant at her interest in him. His eyes narrowed and he smiled. "I was thinking we might take in a movie at one of those big movie complexes in San Antonio. Friday night."

"*Ooooooh,*" she exclaimed, bright-eyed. "I like science fiction."

"So do I, and there's a remake of a 1950's film playing. I wouldn't mind seeing it."

"Neither would I."

"I'll pick you up at your motel about five. We'll have dinner and take in the movie afterward. That suit you?"

She was nodding furiously. "Should I go ahead and buy the rings?" she asked with an innocent expression.

He chuckled. "I told you, I'm too tied up right now for weddings."

She snapped her fingers. "Darn!"

"But we can see a movie."

"I like movies."

"Me, too."

They paid for their respective meals and walked out together, drawing interest from several of the café patrons. Harley hadn't been taking any girls around with him lately, and here was this cute CSI lady from San Antonio having lunch with him. Speculation ran riot.

"They'll have us married by late afternoon," he remarked, nodding toward the windows, where curious eyes were following their every move.

"I'll go back in and invite them all to the wedding, shall I?" she asked at once.

"Kill the engine, dude," he drawled in a perfect imitation of the sea turtle in his favorite cartoon movie.

"You so totally rock, Squirt!" she drawled back.

He laughed. "Sweet. You like cartoon movies, too?"

"Crazy about them," she replied. "My favorite right now is *Wall-E,* but it changes from season to season. They just get better all the time."

"I liked *Wall-E,* too," he agreed. "Poignant story. Beautiful soundtrack."

"My sentiments, exactly. That's nice. When we have kids, we'll enjoy taking them to the theater to see the new cartoon movies."

He took off his hat and started fanning himself. "Don't mention kids or I'll faint!" he exclaimed. "I'm already having hot flashes, just considering the thought of marriage!"

She glared at him. "Women have hot flashes when they enter menopause," she said, emphasizing the first word.

He lifted his eyebrows and grinned. "Maybe I'm a woman in disguise," he whispered wickedly.

She wrinkled her nose up and gave him a slow, interested scrutiny from his cowboy boots to his brown hair. "It's a really good disguise," she had to agree. She growled, low in her throat, and smiled. "Tell you what, after the movie, we can undress you and see how good a disguise it really is."

"Well, I never!" he exclaimed, gasping. "I'm not that kind of man, I'll have you know! And if you keep talking like that, I'll never marry you. A man has his principles. You're just after my body!"

Alice was bursting at the seams with laughter. Harley followed her eyes, turned around, and there was Kilraven, in uniform, staring at him.

"I read this book," Kilraven said after a minute, "about a Scot who disguised himself as a woman for three days after he stole an English payroll destined for the turncoat Scottish Lords of the Congregation who were going to try to depose Mary, Queen of Scots. The family that sheltered him was rewarded with compensation that was paid for centuries, even after his death, they say. He knew how to repay a debt." He frowned. "But that was in the sixteenth century, and you don't look a thing like Lord Bothwell."

"I should hope not," Harley said. "He's been dead for over four hundred years!"

Alice moved close to him and bumped him with her hip. "Don't talk like that. Some of my best friends are dead people."

Harley and Kilraven both groaned.

"It was a joke," Alice burst out, exasperated. "My goodness, don't you people have a sense of humor?"

"He doesn't," Harley said, indicating Kilraven.

"I do so," Kilraven shot back, glaring. "I have a good sense of humor." He stepped closer. "And you'd better say that I do, because I'm armed."

"You have a great sense of humor," Harley replied at once, and grinned.

"What are you doing here?" Alice asked suddenly. "I thought you were supposed to be off today."

Kilraven shrugged. "One of our boys came down with flu and they needed somebody to fill in. Not much to do around here on a day off, so I volunteered," he added.

"There's TV," Alice said.

He scoffed. "I don't own a TV," he said huffily. "I read books."

"European history?" Harley asked, recalling the mention of Bothwell.

"Military history, mostly, but history is history. For instance," he began, "did you know that Hannibal sealed poisonous snakes in clay urns and had his men throw them onto the decks of enemy ships as an offensive measure?"

Harley was trying to keep a straight face.

Alice didn't even try. "You're kidding!"

"I am not. Look it up."

"I'd have gone right over the side into the ocean!" Alice exclaimed, shivering.

"So did a lot of the enemy combatants." Kilraven chuckled. "See what you learn when you read, instead of staying glued to a television set?"

"How can you not have a television set?" Harley exclaimed. "You can't watch the news…"

"Don't get me started," Kilraven muttered. "Corporate news, exploiting private individuals with personal problems for the entertainment of the masses! Look at that murder victim who was killed back in the summer, and the family of the accused is still getting crucified nightly in case they had anything to do with it. You call that news? I call it bread and circuses, just like the arena in ancient Rome!"

"Then how do you know what's going on in the world?" Alice had to know.

"I have a laptop computer with Internet access," he said. "That's where the real news is."

"A revolutionary," Harley said.

"An anarchist," Alice corrected.

"I am an upstanding member of law enforcement," Kilraven retorted. He glanced at the big watch on his wrist. "And I'm going to be late getting back on duty if I don't get lunch pretty soon."

Harley was looking at the watch and frowning. He knew the model. It was one frequently worn by mercs. "Blade or garrote?" he asked Kilraven, nodding at the watch.

Kilraven was surprised, but he recovered quickly. "Blade," he said. "How did you know?"

"Micah Steele used to wear one just like it."

Kilraven leaned down. "Guess who I bought it from?" he asked. He grinned. With a wave, he sauntered into the café.

"What were you talking about?" Alice asked curiously.

"Trade secret," Harley returned. "I have to get going. I'll see you Friday."

He turned away and then, just as suddenly turned back. "Wait a minute." He pulled a small pad and pencil out of his shirt pocket and jotted down a number. He tore off the paper and handed it to her. "That's my cell phone number. If anything comes up, and you can't make it Friday, you can call me."

"Can I call you anyway?" she asked.

He blinked. "What for?"

"To talk. You know, if I have any deeply personal problems that just can't wait until Friday?"

He laughed. "Alice, it's only two days away," he said.

"I could be traumatized by a snake or something."

He sighed. "Okay. But only then. It's hard to pull a cell phone out of its holder when you're knee-deep in mud trying to extract mired cattle."

She beamed. "I'll keep that in mind." She tucked the number in the pocket of her slacks. "I enjoyed lunch."

"Yeah," he said, smiling. "Me, too."

She watched him walk away with covetous eyes. He really did have a sensuous body, very masculine. She stood sighing over him until she realized that several pair of eyes were still watching her from inside the café. With a self-conscious grin in their direction, she went quickly to her van.

The pattern in the tennis shoes was so common that Alice had serious doubts that they'd ever locate the seller, much less the owner. The car was going to be a much better lead. She went up to the crime lab while they were processing it. There was some trace evidence that was promising. She also had Sergeant Rick Marquez, who worked out of San Antonio P.D., get as much information as he could about the woman the murdered man had stolen the car from.

The next morning in Jacobsville, on his way to work in San Antonio, Rick stopped by Alice's motel room to give her the information he'd managed to obtain. "She's been an employee of Senator Fowler for about two years," Rick said, perching on the edge of the dresser in front of the bed while she paced. "She's deeply religious. She goes to church on Sundays and Wednesdays. She's involved in an outreach program for the homeless, and she gives away a good deal of her salary to people she considers more needy." He shook his head. "You read about these people, but you rarely encounter them in real life. She hasn't got a black mark on her record anywhere, unless you consider a detention in high school for being late three days in a row when her mother was in the hospital."

"Wow," Alice exclaimed softly.

"There's more. She almost lost the job by lecturing the senator for hiring illegal workers and threatening them with deportation if they asked for higher wages."

"What a sweetheart," Alice muttered.

"From what we hear, the senator is the very devil to work for. They say his wife is almost as hard-nosed. She was a state supreme court judge before she went into the import/export business. She made millions at it. Finances a good part of the senator's reelection campaigns."

"Is he honest?"

"Is any politician?" Marquez asked cynically. "He sits on several powerful committees in Congress, and was once accused of taking kickbacks from a Mexican official."

"For what?"

"He was asked to oppose any shoring up of border security. Word is that the senator and his contact have their fingers in some illegal pies, most notably drug trafficking. But there's no proof. The last detective who tried to investigate the senator is now working traffic detail."

"A vengeful man."

"Very."

"I don't suppose that detective would talk to me?" she wondered aloud.

"She might," he replied surprisingly. "She and I were trying to get the Kilraven family murder case reopened, if you recall, when pressure was put on us to stop. She turned her attention to the senator and got kicked out of the detective squad." He grimaced. "She's a good woman. Got an invalid kid to look after and an ex-husband who's a pain in the butt, to put it nicely."

"We heard about the cold case being closed. You think the senator might have been responsible for it?" she wondered aloud.

"We don't know. He has a protégé who's just been elected junior senator from Texas, and the protégé has some odd ties to people who aren't exactly the crème of society. But we don't dare mention that in public." He smiled. "I don't fancy being put on a motorcycle at my age and launched into traffic duty."

"Your friend isn't having to do that, surely?" she asked.

"No, she's working two-car patrols on the night shift, but she's a sergeant, so she gets a good bit of desk work." He studied her. "What's this I hear about you trying to marry Harley?"

She grinned. "It's early days. He's shy, but I'm going to drown him in flowers and chocolate until he says yes."

"Good luck," he said with a chuckle.

"I won't even need it. We're going to a movie together Friday."

"Are you? What are you going to see?"

"The remake of that fifties movie. We're going to dinner first."

"You are a fast worker, Alice," he said with respect. He checked his watch. "I've got to get back to the precinct."

She glanced at his watch curiously. "You don't have a blade or a wire in that thing, do you?"

"Not likely," he assured her. "Those watches cost more than I make, and they're used almost exclusively by mercs."

"Mercs?" She frowned.

"Soldiers of fortune. They work for the highest bidder, although our local crowd had more honor than that."

Mercs. Now she understood Harley's odd phrasing about "trade secrets."

"Where did you see a watch like that?" he asked.

She looked innocent. "I heard about one from Harley. I just wondered what they were used for."

"Oh. Well, I guess if you were in a tight spot, it might save your life to have one of those," he agreed, distracted.

"Before you go, can you give me the name and address of that detective in San Antonio?" she asked.

He hesitated. "Better let me funnel the questions to her, Alice," he said with a smile. "She doesn't want anything to slip out about her follow-ups on that case. She's still working it, without permission."

She raised an eyebrow. "So are you, unless I miss my guess. Does Kilraven know?"

He shook his head. Then he hesitated. "Well, I don't think he does. He and Jon Blackhawk still don't want us nosing around. They're afraid the media will pick up the story and it will become the nightly news for a year or so." He shook his head. "Pitiful, how the networks don't go out and get any real news anymore. They just create it by harping on private families mixed up in tragedies, like living soap operas."

"That's how corporate media works," she told him. "If you want real news, buy a local weekly newspaper."

He laughed. "You're absolutely right. Take care, Alice."

"You, too. Thanks for the help."

"Anytime." He paused at the door and grinned at her. "If Harley doesn't work out, you could always pursue me," he invited. "I'm young and dashing and I even have long hair." He indicated his ponytail. "I played semiprofessional soccer when I was in college, and I have a lovely singing voice."

She chuckled. "I've heard about your singing voice, Marquez. Weren't you asked, very politely, to stay out of the church choir?"

"I wanted to meet women," he said. "The choir was full of unattached ones. But I can sing," he added belligerently. "Some people don't appreciate real talent."

She wasn't touching that line with a pole. "I'll keep you in mind."

"You do that." He laughed as he closed the door.

Alice turned back to her notes, spread out on the desk in the motel room. There was something nagging at her about the piece of paper they'd recovered from the murder victim. She wondered why it bothered her.

Harley picked her up punctually at five on Friday night for their date. He wasn't overdressed, but he had on slacks and a spotless sports shirt with a dark blue jacket. He wasn't wearing his cowboy hat, either.

"You look nice," she said, smiling.

His eyes went to her neat blue sweater with embroidery around the rounded neckline and the black slacks she was wearing with slingbacks. She draped a black coat with fur collar over one arm and picked up her purse.

"Thanks," he said. "You look pretty good yourself, Alice."

She joined him at the door. "Ooops. Just a minute. I forgot my cell phone. I was charging it."

She unplugged it and tucked it into her pocket. It rang immediately. She grimaced. "Just a minute, okay?" she asked Harley.

She answered the phone. She listened. She grimaced. "Not tonight," she groaned. "Listen, I have plans. I never do, but I really have plans tonight. Can't Clancy cover for me, just this once? Please? Pretty please? I'll do the same for her. I'll even work Christmas Eve…okay? Thanks!" She beamed. "Thanks a million!"

She hung up.

"A case?" he asked curiously.

"Yes, but I traded out with another investigator." She shook her head as she joined him again at the door. "It's been so slow lately that I forgot how hectic my life usually is."

"You have to work Christmas Eve?" he asked, surprised.

"Well, I usually volunteer," she confessed. "I don't have much of a social life. Besides, I think parents should be with children on holidays. I don't have any, but all my coworkers do."

He paused at the door of his pickup truck and looked down at her. "I like kids," he said.

"So do I," she replied seriously, and without joking. "I've just never had the opportunity to become a parent."

"You don't have to be married to have kids," he pointed out.

She gave him a harsh glare. "I am the product of generations of Baptist ministers," she told him. "My father was the only one of five brothers who went into business instead. You try having a modern attitude with a mother who taught Sunday School and uncles who spent their lives counseling young women whose lives were destroyed by unexpected pregnancies."

"I guess it would be rough," he said.

She smiled. "You grew up with parents who were free thinkers, didn't you?" she asked, curious.

He grimaced. He put her into the truck and got in beside her before he answered. "My father is an agnostic. He doesn't believe in anything except the power of the almighty dollar. My mother is just like him. They wanted me to associate with the right people and help them do it. I stayed with a friend's parents for a while and all but got adopted by them—he was a mechanic and they had a small ranch. I helped in the mechanic's shop. Then I went into the service, came back and tried to work things out with my real parents, but it wasn't possible. I ran away from home, fresh out of the Army Rangers."

"You were overseas during the Bosnia conflict, weren't you?" she asked.

He snapped his seat belt a little violently. "I was a desk clerk," he said with disgust. "I washed out of combat training. I couldn't make the grade. I ended up back in the regular Army doing clerical jobs. I never even saw combat. Not in the Army," he added.

"Oh."

"I left home, came down here to become a cowboy barely knowing a cow from a bull. The friends that I lived with had a small ranch, but I mostly stayed in town, working at the shop. We went out to the ranch on weekends, and I wasn't keen on livestock back then. Mr. Parks took me on anyway. He knew all along that I had no experience, but he put me to work with an old veteran cowhand named Cal Lucas who taught me everything I know about cattle."

She grinned. "It took guts to do that."

He laughed. "I guess so. I bluffed a lot, although I am a good mechanic. Then I got in with this Sunday merc crew and went down to Africa with them one week on a so-called training mission. All we did was talk to some guys in a village about their problems with foreign relief shipments. But before we could do anything, we ran afoul of government troops and got sent home." He sighed. "I bragged about how much I'd learned, what a great merc I was." He glanced at her as they drove toward San Antonio, but she wasn't reacting critically. Much the reverse. He relaxed a little. "Then one of the drug lords came storming up to Mr. Parks's house with his men and I got a dose of reality—an automatic in my face. Mr. Parks jerked two combat knives out of his sleeves and threw them at the two men who were holding me. Put them both down in a heartbeat." He shook his head, still breathless at the memory. "I never saw anything like it, before or since. I thought he was just a rancher. Turns out he went with Micah Steele and Eb Scott on real merc missions overseas. He listened to me brag and watched me strut, and never said a word. I'd never have known, if the drug dealers hadn't attacked. We got in a firefight with them later."

"We heard about that, even up in San Antonio," she said.

He nodded. "It got around. Mr. Parks and Eb Scott and Micah Steele got together to take out a drug distribution center near Mr. Parks's property. I swallowed my pride and asked to go along. They let me." He sighed. "I grew up in the space of an hour. I saw men shot and killed, I had my life saved by Mr. Parks again in the process. Afterward, I never bragged or strutted again. Mr. Parks said he was proud of me." He flushed a little. "If my father had been like him, I guess I'd still be at home. He's a real man, Mr. Parks. I've never known a better one."

"He likes you, too."

He laughed self-consciously. "He does. He's offered me a few acres of land and some cattle, if I'd like to start my own herd. I'm thinking about it. I love ranching. I think I'm getting good at it."

"So we'd live on a cattle ranch." She pursed her lips mischievously. "I guess I could learn to help with branding. I mean, we wouldn't want our kids to think their mother was a sissy, would we?" she asked, laughing.

Harley gave her a sideways glance and grinned. She really was fun to be with. He thought he might take her by the ranch one day while she was still in Jacobsville and introduce her to Mr. Parks. He was sure Mr. Parks would like her.

Five

The restaurant Harley took Alice to was a very nice one, with uniformed waiters and chandeliers.

"Oh, Harley, this wasn't necessary," she said quickly, flushing. "A hamburger would have been fine!"

He smiled. "We all got a Christmas bonus from Mr. Parks," he explained. "I don't drink or smoke or gamble, so I can afford a few luxuries from time to time."

"You don't have any vices? Wow. Now I really think we should set the date." She glanced at him under her lashes. "I don't drink, smoke or gamble, either," she added hopefully.

He nodded. "We'll be known as the most prudish couple in Jacobsville."

"Kilraven's prudish, too," she pointed out.

"Yes, but he won't be living in Jacobsville much

longer. He's been reassigned, we're hearing. After all, he's really a fed."

She studied the menu. "I'll bet he could be a heartbreaker with a little practice."

"He's breaking Winnie Sinclair's heart, anyway, by leaving," Harley said, repeating the latest gossip. "She's really got a case on him. But he thinks she's too young."

"He's only in his thirties," she pointed out.

"Yes, but Winnie's the same age as her brother's new wife," he replied. "Boone Sinclair thought Keely Welsh was too young for him, too."

"But he gave in, in the end. You know, the Ballenger brothers in Jacobsville both married younger women. They've been happy together, all these years."

"Yes, they have."

The waiter came and took their orders. Alice had a shrimp cocktail and a large salad with coffee. Harley gave her a curious look.

"Aren't you hungry?" he asked.

She laughed. "I told you in Jacobsville, I love salads," she confessed. "I mostly eat them at every meal." She indicated her slender body. "I guess that's how I keep the weight off."

"I can eat as much as I like. I run it all off," he replied. "Working cattle is not for the faint of heart or the out-of-condition rancher."

She grinned. "I believe it." She smiled at the waiter as he deposited coffee in their china cups and left. "Why did you want to be a cowboy?" she asked him.

"I loved old Western movies on satellite," he said simply. "Gary Cooper and John Wayne and Randolph Scott. I dreamed of living on a cattle ranch and having animals around. I don't even mind washing Bob when she gets dirty, or Puppy Dog."

"What's Puppy Dog's name?" she asked.

"Puppy Dog."

She gave him an odd look. "Who's on first, what's on second, I don't know's on third?"

"I don't give a damn's our shortstop?" he finished the old Abbott and Costello comedy routine. He laughed. "No, it's not like that. His name really is Puppy Dog. We have a guy in town, Tom Walker. He had an outlandish dog named Moose that saved his daughter from a rattlesnake. Moose sired a litter of puppies. Moose is dead now, but Puppy Dog, who was one of his offspring, went to live with Lisa Monroe, before she married my boss. She called him Puppy Dog and figured it was as good a name as any. With a girl dog named Bob, my boss could hardly disagree," he added on a chuckle.

"I see."

"Do you like animals?"

"I love them," she said. "But I can't have animals in the apartment building where I live. I had cats and dogs and even a parrot when I lived at home."

"Do you have family?"

She shook her head. "My dad was the only one left. He died a few months ago. I have uncles, but we're not close."

"Did you love your parents?"

She smiled warmly. "Very much. My dad was a banker. We went fishing together on weekends. My mother was a housewife who never wanted to run a corporation or be a professional. She just wanted a houseful of kids, but I was the only child she was able to have. She spoiled me rotten. Dad tried to counterbalance her." She sipped coffee. "I miss them both. I wish I'd had brothers or sisters." She looked at him. "Do you have siblings?"

"I had a sister," he said quietly.

"Had?"

He nodded. He fingered his coffee cup. "She died when she was seven years old."

She hesitated. He looked as if this was a really bad memory. "How?"

He smiled sadly. "My father backed over her on his way down the driveway, in a hurry to get to a meeting."

She grimaced. "Poor man."

He cocked his head and studied her. "Why do you say that?"

"We had a little girl in for autopsy, about two years ago," she began. "Her dad was hysterical. Said the television fell over on her." She lifted her eyes. "You know, we don't just take someone's word for how an accident happens, even if we believe it. We run tests to check out the explanation and make sure it's feasible. Well, we pushed over a television of the same size as the one in the dad's apartment. Sure enough, it did catastrophic damage to a dummy." She shook her head. "Poor man went crazy. I mean, he really lost the will to live. His wife had died. The child was all he had left. He locked himself in the bathroom with a shotgun one night and pulled the trigger with his toe." She made a harsh sound. "Not the sort of autopsy you want to try to sleep after."

He was frowning.

"Sorry," she said, wincing. "I tend to talk shop. I know it's sickening, and here we are in a nice restaurant and all, and I did pour a glass of tea on a guy this week for doing the same thing to me…"

"I was thinking about the father," he said, smiling to

relieve her tension. "I was sixteen when it happened. I grieved for her, of course, but my life was baseball and girls and video games and hamburgers. I never considered how my father might have felt. He seemed to just get on with his life afterward. So did my mother."

"Lots of people may seem to get over their grief. They don't."

He was more thoughtful than ever. "My mother had been a…lawyer," he said after a slight hesitation that Alice didn't notice. "She was very correct and proper. After my sister died, she changed. Cocktail parties, the right friends, the best house, the fanciest furniture…she went right off the deep end."

"You didn't connect it?"

He grimaced. "That was when I ran away from home and went to live with the mechanic and his wife," he confessed. "It was my senior year of high school. I graduated soon after, went into the Army and served for two years. When I got out, I went home. But I only stayed for a couple of weeks. My parents were total strangers. I didn't even know them anymore."

"That's sad. Do you have any contact with them?"

He shook his head. "I just left. They never even looked for me."

She slid her hand impulsively over his. His fingers turned and enveloped hers. His light blue eyes searched her darker ones curiously. "I never thought of crime scene investigators as having feelings," he said. "I thought you had to be pretty cold-blooded to do that sort of thing."

She smiled. "I'm the last hope of the doomed," she said. "The conscience of the murdered. The flickering candle of the soul of the deceased. I do my job so that murderers don't flourish, so that killers don't escape justice. I think of my job as a holy grail," she said solemnly. "I hide my feelings. But I still have them. It hurts to see a life extinguished. Any life. But especially a child's."

His eyes began to twinkle with affection. "Alice, you're one of a kind."

"Oh, I do hope so," she said after a minute. "Because if there was another one of me, I might lose my job. Not many people would give twenty-four hours a day to the work." She hesitated and grinned. "Well, not all the time, obviously. Just occasionally, I get taken out by handsome, dashing men."

He laughed. "Thanks."

"Actually I mean it. I'm not shrewd enough to lie well."

The waiter came and poured more coffee and took their orders for dessert. When they were eating it, Alice frowned thoughtfully.

"It bothers me."

"What does?" he asked.

"The car. Why would a man steal a car from an upstanding, religious woman and then get killed?"

"He didn't know he was going to get killed."

She forked a piece of cheesecake and looked at it. "What if he had a criminal record? What if he got involved with her and wanted to change, to start over? What if he had something on his conscience and he wanted to spill the beans?" She looked up. "And somebody involved knew it and had to stop him?"

"That's a lot of if's," he pointed out.

She nodded. "Yes, it is. We still don't know who the car was driven by, and the woman's story that it was stolen is just a little thin." She put the fork down. "I want to talk to her. But I don't know how to go about it. She works for a dangerous politician, I'm told. The feds have backed off. I won't do myself any favors if I charge in and start interrogating the senator's employee."

He studied her. "Let me see if I can find a way. I used to know my way around political circles. Maybe I can help."

She laughed. "You know a U.S. senator?" she teased.

He pursed his lips. "Maybe I know somebody who's related to one," he corrected.

"It would really help me a lot, if I could get to her before the feds do. I think she might tell me more than she'd tell a no-nonsense man."

"Give me until tomorrow. I'll think of something."

She smiled. "You're a doll."

He chuckled. "So are you."

She flushed. "Thanks."

They exchanged a long, soulful glance, only interrupted by the arrival of the waiter to ask if they wanted anything else and present the check. Alice's heart was doing double-time on the way out of the restaurant.

Harley walked her to the door of the motel. "I had a good time," he told her. "The best I've had in years."

She looked up, smiling. "Me, too. I turn off most men. The job, you know. I do work with people who aren't breathing."

"It doesn't matter," he said.

She felt the same tension that was visible in his tall, muscular body. He moved a step closer. She met him halfway.

He bent and drew his mouth softly over hers. When she didn't object, his arms went around her and pulled her close. He smiled as he increased the gentle pressure of his lips and felt hers tremble just a little before they relaxed and answered the pressure.

His body was already taut with desire, but it was too soon for a heated interlude. He didn't want to rush her. She was the most fascinating woman he'd ever known. He had to go slow.

He drew back after a minute and his hands tightened on her arms. "Suppose we take in another movie next week?" he asked.

She brightened. "A whole movie?"

He laughed softly. "At least."

"I'd like that."

"We'll try another restaurant. Just to sample the ones that are available until we find one we approve of," he teased.

"What a lovely idea! We can write reviews and put them online, too."

He pursed his lips. "What an entertaining thought."

"Nice reviews," she said, divining his mischievous thoughts.

"Spoilsport."

He winked at her, and she blushed.

"Don't forget," she said. "About finding me a way to interview that woman, okay?"

"Okay," he said. "Good night."

"Good night."

She stood, sighing, as he walked back to his truck. But when he got inside and started it, he didn't drive away. She realized belatedly that he was waiting until she went inside and locked the door. She laughed and waved. She liked that streak of protectiveness in him. It might not be modern, but it certainly made her feel cherished. She slept like a charm.

* * *

The next morning, he called her on his cell phone before she left the motel. "I've got us invited to a cocktail party tonight," he told her. "A fundraiser for the senator."

"Us? But we can't contribute to that sort of thing! Can we?" she added.

"We don't have to. We're representing a contributor who's out of the country," he added with a chuckle. "Do you have a nice cocktail dress?"

"I do, but it's in San Antonio, in my apartment."

"No worries. You can go up and get it and I'll pick you up there at six."

"Fantastic! I'll wear something nice and I won't burp the theme songs to any television shows," she promised.

"Oh, that's good to know," he teased. "Got to get back to work. I told Mr. Parks I had to go to San Antonio this afternoon, so he's giving me a half day off. I didn't tell him why I needed the vacation time, but I think he suspects something."

"Don't mention this to anybody else, okay?" she asked. "If Jon Blackhawk or Kilraven find out, my goose will be cooked."

"I won't tell a soul."

"See you later. I owe you one, Harley."

"Yes," he drawled softly. "You do, don't you? I'll phone you later and get directions to your apartment."

"Okay."

She laughed and hung up.

The senator lived in a mansion. It was two stories high, with columns, and it had a front porch bigger than Alice's whole apartment. Lights burned in every room, and in the gloomy, rainy night, it looked welcoming and beautiful.

Luxury sedans were parked up and down the driveway. Harley's pickup truck wasn't in the same class, but he didn't seem to feel intimidated. He parked on the street and helped Alice out of the truck. He was wearing evening clothes, with a black bow tie and highly polished black wingtip shoes. He looked elegant. Alice was wearing a simple black cocktail dress with her best winter coat, the one she wore to work, a black one with a fur collar. She carried her best black evening bag and she wore black pumps that she'd polished, hoping to cover the scuff marks. On her salary, although it was a good one, she could hardly afford haute couture.

They were met at the door by a butler in uniform. Harley handed him an invitation and the man hesitated and did a double take, but he didn't say anything.

Once they were inside, Alice looked worriedly at Harley.

"It's okay," he assured her, smiling as he cradled her hand in his protectively. "No problem."

"Gosh," she said, awestruck as she looked around her at the company she was in. "There's a movie star over there," she said under her breath. "I recognize at least two models and a Country-Western singing star, and there's the guy who won the golf tournament...!"

"They're just people, Alice," he said gently.

She gaped at him. "Just people? You're joking, right?" She turned too fast and bumped into somebody. She looked up to apologize and her eyes almost popped. "S-sorry," she stammered.

A movie star with a martial arts background grinned at her. "No problem. It's easy to get knocked down in here. What a crowd, huh?"

"Y-yes," she agreed, nodding.

He laughed, smiled at Harley, and drew his date, a gorgeous blonde, along with him toward the buffet table.

Harley curled his fingers into Alice's. "Rube," he teased softly. "You're starstruck."

"I am, I am," she agreed at once. "I've never been in such a place in my life. I don't hang out with the upper echelons of society in my job. You seem very much at home," she added, "for a man who spends his time with horses and cattle."

"Not a bad analogy, actually," he said under his breath. "Wouldn't a cattle prod come in handy around here, though?"

"Harley!" She laughed.

"Just kidding." He was looking around the room. After a minute, he spotted someone. "Let's go ask that woman if they know your employee."

"Okay."

"What's her name?" he whispered.

She dug for it. "Dolores."

He slid his arm around her shoulders and led her forward. She felt the warmth of his jacketed arm around her with real pleasure. She felt chilled at this party, with all this elegance. Her father had been a banker, and he hadn't been poor, but this was beyond the dreams of most people. Crystal chandeliers, Persian carpets, original oil paintings—was that a Renoir?!

"Hi," Harley said to one of the women pouring more punch into the Waterford crystal bowl. "Does Dolores still work here?"

The woman stared at him for a minute, but without recognition. "Dolores? Yes. She's in the kitchen, making canapés. You look familiar. Do I know you?"

"I've got that kind of face," he said easily, smiling.

"My wife and I know Dolores, we belong to her church. I promised the minister we'd give her a message from him if we came tonight," he added.

"One of that church crowd," the woman groaned, rolling her eyes. "Honestly, it's all she talks about, like there's nothing else in the world but church."

"Religion dies, so does civilization," Alice said quietly. She remembered that from her Western Civilization course in college.

"Whatever," the woman replied, bored.

"In the kitchen, huh? Thanks," Harley told the woman.

"Don't get her fired," came the quick reply. "She's a pain, sometimes, but she works hard enough doing dishes. If the senator or his wife see you keeping her from her job, he'll fire her."

"We won't do that," Harley promised. His lips made a thin line as he led Alice away.

"Surely the senator wouldn't fire her just for talking to us?" Alice wondered aloud.

"It wouldn't surprise me," Harley said. "We'll have to be circumspect."

Alice followed his lead. She wondered why he was so irritated. Perhaps the woman's remark offended his sense of justice.

The kitchen was crowded. It didn't occur to Alice to ask how Harley knew his way there. Women were bent over tables, preparing platters, sorting food, making canapés. Two women were at the huge double sink, washing dishes.

"Don't they have a dishwasher?" Alice wondered as they entered the room.

"You don't put Waterford crystal and Lenox china in a dishwasher," he commented easily.

She looked up at him with pure fascination. He didn't seem aware that he'd given away knowledge no working cowboy should even possess.

"How do we know which one's her?" he asked Alice.

Alice stared at the two women. One was barely out of her teens, wearing a nose ring and spiky hair. The other was conservatively dressed with her hair in a neat bun. She smiled, nodding toward the older one. She had a white apron wrapped around her. "The other woman said she was washing dishes," she whispered. "And she's a churchgoer."

He grinned, following her lead.

They eased around the curious workers, smiling.

"Hello, Dolores," Alice called to the woman.

The older woman turned, her red hands dripping water and soap, and started at the two visitors with wide brown eyes. "I'm sorry, do I know you?" she asked.

"I guess you've never seen us dressed up, huh? We're from your church," he told her, lying through his teeth. "Your minister gave us a message for you."

She blinked. "My minister…?"

"Could we talk, just for a minute?" Alice asked urgently.

The woman was suspicious. Her eyes narrowed. She hesitated, and Alice thought, *we've blown it.* But just then, Dolores nodded. "Sure. We can talk for a minute. Liz, I'm taking my break, now, okay? I'll only be ten minutes."

"Okay," Liz returned, with only a glance at the elegantly dressed people walking out with Dolores. "Don't be long. You know how he is," she added quickly.

Once they were outside, Dolores gave them a long look. "I know everyone in my church. You two don't go there," Dolores said with a gleam in her eyes. "Who are you and what do you want?"

Alice studied her. "I work for…out-of-town law enforcement," she improvised. "We found your car. And the man who was driving it."

The older woman hesitated. "I told the police yesterday, the car was stolen," she began weakly.

Alice stepped close, so that they couldn't be overheard. "He was beaten to death, so badly that his mother wouldn't know him," she said in a steely tone. "Your car was pushed into the river. Somebody didn't want him to be found. Nobody," she added softly, "should ever have to die like that. And his murderer shouldn't get away with it."

Dolores looked even sicker. She leaned back against the wall. Her eyes closed. "It's my fault. He said he wanted to start over. He wanted to marry me. He said he just had to do something first, to get something off his conscience. He asked to borrow the car, but he said if something happened, if he didn't call me back by the next morning, to say it was stolen so I wouldn't get in trouble. He said he knew about a crime and if he talked they might kill him."

"Do you know what crime?" Alice asked her.

She shook her head. "He wouldn't tell me anything. Nothing. He said it was the only way he could protect me."

"His name," Alice persisted. "Can you at least tell me his name?"

Dolores glanced toward the door, grimacing. "I don't know it," she whispered. "He said it was an alias."

"Then tell me the alias. Help me find his killer."

She drew in a breath. "Jack. Jack Bailey," she said. "He

said he'd been in jail once. He said he was sorry. I got him going to church, trying to live a decent life. He was going to start over…" Her voice broke. "It's my fault."

"You were helping him," Alice corrected. "You gave him hope."

"He's dead."

"Yes. But there are worse things than dying. How long did you know him?" Alice asked.

"A few months. We went out together. He didn't own a car. I had to drive…"

"Where did he live?"

Dolores glanced at the door again. "I don't know. He always met me at a little strip mall near the tracks, the Weston Street Mall."

"Is there anything you can tell me that might help identify him?" Alice asked.

She blinked, deep in thought. "He said something happened, that it was an accident, but people died because of it. He was sorry. He said it was time to tell the truth, no matter how dangerous it was to him…"

"Dolores!"

She jumped. A tall, imposing figure stood in the light from the open door. "Get back in here! You aren't paid to socialize."

Harley stiffened, because he knew that voice.

"Yes, sir!" Dolores cried, rushing back inside. "Sorry. I was on my break…!"

She ran past the elegant older man. He closed the door and came storming toward Alice and Harley, looking as if he meant to start trouble.

"What do you mean, interrupting my workers when I have important guests? Who the hell are you people and how did you get in here?" he demanded.

Harley moved into the light, his pale eyes glittering at the older man. "I had an invitation," he said softly.

The older man stopped abruptly. He cocked his head, as if the voice meant more to him than the face did. "Who…are you?" he asked huskily.

"Just a ghost, visiting old haunts," he said, and there was ice in his tone.

The older man moved a step closer. As he came into the light, Alice noticed that he, too, had pale eyes, and gray-streaked brown hair.

"H-Harley?" he asked in a hesitant tone.

Harley caught Alice's hand in his. She noticed that his fingers were like ice.

"Sorry to have bothered you, Senator," Harley said formally. "Alice and I know a pastor who's a mutual friend of Dolores. He asked us to tell her about a family that needed a ride to church Sunday. Please excuse us."

He drew Alice around the older man, who stood frozen watching them as they went back into the kitchen.

Harley paused by Dolores and whispered something in her ear quickly before he rejoined Alice and they sauntered toward the living room. The senator moved toward them before they reached the living room, stared after them with a pained expression and tried to speak.

It was too late. Harley walked Alice right out the front door. On the way, a dark-eyed, dark-haired man in an expensive suit scowled as they passed him. Harley noticed that the senator stopped next to the other man and started talking to him.

They made it back to the truck without being challenged, and without a word being spoken.

Harley put Alice inside the truck, got in and started it.

"He knew you," she stammered.

"Apparently." He nodded at her. "Fasten your seat belt."

"Sure." She snapped it in place, hoping that he might add something, explain what had happened. He didn't.

"You've got something to go on now, at least," he said.

"Yes," she agreed. "I have. Thanks, Harley. Thanks very much."

"My pleasure." He glanced at her. "I told Dolores what we said to the senator, so that our stories would match. It might save her job."

"I hope so," she said. "She seemed like a really nice person."

"Yeah."

He hardly said two words the whole rest of the way to her apartment. He parked in front of the building.

"You coming back down to Jacobsville?" he asked.

"In the morning," she said. "I still have some investigating to do there."

"Lunch, Monday, at Barbara's?" he invited.

She smiled. "I'd like that."

He smiled back. "Yeah. Me, too. Sorry we didn't get to stay. The buffet looked pretty good."

"I wasn't really hungry," she lied.

"You're a sweetheart. I'd take you out for a late supper, but my heart's not in it." He pulled her close and bent to kiss her. His mouth was hard and a little rough. "Thanks for not asking questions."

"No problem," she managed, because the kiss had been something, even if he hadn't quite realized what he was doing.

"See you Monday."

He went back to the truck and drove away. This time, he didn't wait for her to go in and close the door, an indication of how upset he really was.

Six

Harley drove back to the ranch and cut off the engine outside the bunkhouse. It had been almost eight years since he'd seen the senator. He hadn't realized what a shock it was going to be, to come face-to-face with him. It brought back all the old wounds.

"Hey!"

He glanced at the porch of the modern bunkhouse. Charlie Dawes was staring at him from a crack in the door. "You coming in or sleeping out there?" the other cowboy called with a laugh.

"Coming in, I guess," he replied.

"Well!" Charlie exclaimed when he saw how the other man was dressed. "I thought you said you were just going out for a drive."

"I took Alice to a party, but we left early. Neither of us was in the mood," he said.

"Alice. That your girl?"

Harley smiled. "You know," he told the other man, "I think she is."

Alice drove back down to Jacobsville late Sunday afternoon. She'd contacted Rick Marquez and asked if he'd do some investigating for her in San Antonio, to look for any rap sheet on a man who used a Jack Bailey alias and to see if they could find a man who'd been staying at a motel near the Weston Street Mall. He might have been seen in the company of a dark-haired woman driving a 1992 blue Ford sedan. It wasn't much to go on, but he might turn up something.

Meanwhile, Alice was going to go back to the crime scene and wander over it one more time, in hopes that the army of CSI detectives might have missed something, some tiny scrap of information that would help break the case.

She was dressed in jeans and sneakers and a green sweatshirt with CSI on it, sweeping the bank of the river, when her cell phone rang. She muttered as she pulled it out and checked the number. She frowned. Odd, she didn't recognize that number in any conscious way, but it struck something in the back of her mind.

"Jones," she said.

"Hi, Jones. It's Kilraven. I wondered if you dug up anything on the murder victim over the weekend?"

She sighed, her mind still on the ground she was searching. "Only that he had an alias, that he was trying to get something off his conscience, that he didn't own a car and he'd been in trouble with the law. Oh, and that he lived somewhere near the Weston Street Mall in San Antonio."

"Good God!" he exclaimed. "You got all that in one weekend?"

She laughed self-consciously. "Well, Harley helped. We crashed a senator's fundraiser and cornered an employee of his who'd been dating the… Oh, damn!" she exclaimed. "Listen, your brother will fry me up toasty and feed me to sharks if you tell him I said that. The feds didn't want anybody going near that woman!"

"Relax. Jon was keen to go out and talk to her himself, but his office nixed it. They were just afraid that some heavy-handed lawman would go over there and spook her. You share what you just told me with him, and I guarantee nobody will say a word about it. Great work, Alice."

"Thanks," she said. "The woman's name is Dolores. She's a nice lady. She feels guilty that he got killed. She never even fussed about her car and now it's totaled. She said she loaned him the car, but he told her to say it was stolen if he didn't call her in a day, in case somebody went after him. He knew he could get killed."

"He said he wanted to get something off his conscience," he reminded her.

"Yes. He said something happened that was an accident but that people died because of it. Does that help?"

"Only if I had ESP," he sighed. "Any more luck on that piece of paper you found in the victim's hand?"

"None. I hope to hear something in a few days from the lab. They're working their fingers to the bone. Why are holidays such a great time for murders and suicides?" she wondered aloud. "It's the holidays. You'd think it would make people happy."

"Sadly, as we both know, it doesn't. It just emphasizes what they've lost, since holidays are prime time for families to get together."

"I suppose so."

"We heard that you were going out with Harley Fowler," he said after a minute, with laughter in his deep voice. "Is it serious?"

"Not really," she replied pertly. "I mean, I ask him to marry me twice a day, but that's not what you'd call serious, is it?"

"Only if he says yes," he returned.

"He hasn't yet, but it's still early. I'm very persistent."

"Well, good luck."

"I don't need luck. I'm unspeakably beautiful, have great language skills, I can boil eggs and wash cars and… Hello? Hello!"

He'd hung up on her, laughing. She closed the flip phone. "I didn't want to talk to you, anyway," she told the phone. "I'm trying to work here."

She walked along the riverbank again, her sharp eyes on the rocks and weeds that grew along the water's edge. She was letting her mind wander, not trying to think in any conscious way. Sometimes, she got ideas that way.

The dead man had a past. He was mixed up in some sort of accident in which a death occurred that caused more deaths. He wanted to get something off his conscience. So he'd borrowed a car from his girlfriend and driven to Jacobsville. To see whom? The town wasn't that big, but it was pretty large if you were trying to figure out who someone a man with a criminal past was trying to find. Who could it be? Someone in law enforcement? Or was he just driving through Jacobsville on his way to talk to someone?

No, she discarded that possibility immediately. He'd

been killed here, so someone had either intercepted him or met him here, to talk about the past.

The problem was, she didn't have a clue who the man was or what he'd been involved in. She hoped that Rick Marquez came up with some answers.

But she knew more than she'd known a few days earlier, at least, and so did law enforcement. She still wondered at the interest of Jon Blackhawk of the San Antonio FBI office. Why were the feds involved? Were they working on some case secretly and didn't want to spill the beans to any outsiders?

Maybe they were working a similar case, she reasoned, and were trying to find a connection. They'd never tell her, of course, but she was a trained professional and this wasn't her first murder investigation.

What if the dead man had confessed, first, to the minister of Dolores's church?

She gasped out loud. It was like lightning striking. Of course! The minister might know something that he could tell her, unless he'd taken a vow of silence, like Catholic priests. They couldn't divulge anything learned in the confessional. But it was certainly worth a try!

She dug Harley's cell phone number out of her pocket and called him. The phone rang three times while she kicked at a dirt clod impatiently. Maybe he was knee-deep in mired cattle or something…

"Hello?"

"Harley!" she exclaimed.

"Now, just who else would it be, talking on Harley's phone?" came the amused, drawling reply.

"You, I hope," she said at once. "Listen, I need to talk to you…"

"You are," he reminded her.

"No, in person, right now," she emphasized. "It's about a minister..."

"Darlin', we can't get married today," he drawled. "I have to brush Bob the dog's teeth," he added lightly.

"Not that minister," she burst out. "Dolores's minister!"

He paused. "Why?"

"What if the murdered man confessed to him before he drove down to Jacobsville and got killed?" she exclaimed.

Harley whistled. "What if, indeed?"

"We need to go talk to her again and ask his name."

"Oh, now that may prove difficult. There's no party."

She realized that he was right. They had no excuse to show up at the senator's home, which was probably surrounded by security devices and armed guards. "Damn!"

"You can just call the house and ask for Dolores," he said reasonably. "You don't have to give your name or a reason."

She laughed softly. "Yes, I could do that. I don't know why I bothered you."

"Because you want to marry me," he said reasonably. "But I'm brushing the dog's teeth today. Sorry."

She glared at the phone. "Excuses, excuses," she muttered. "I'm growing older by the minute!"

"Why don't I bring you over here to go riding?" he wondered aloud. "You could meet my boss and his wife and the boys, and meet Puppy Dog."

She brightened. "What a nice idea!"

"I thought so myself. I'll ask the boss. Next weekend, maybe? I'll beg for another half day on Saturday and take you riding around the ranch. We've got plenty of spare horses." When she hesitated, he sighed. "Don't tell me. You can't ride."

"I can so ride horses," she said indignantly. "I ride horses at amusement parks all the time. They go up and down and round and round, and music plays."

"That isn't the same sort of riding. Well, I'll teach you," he said. "After all, if we get married, you'll have to live on a ranch. I'm not stuffing myself into some tiny apartment in San Antonio."

"Now that's the sort of talk I love to hear," she sighed.

He laughed. "Wear jeans and boots," he instructed. "And thick socks."

"No blouse or bra?" she exclaimed in mock outrage.

He whistled. "Well, you don't have to wear them on my account," he said softly. "But we wouldn't want to shock my boss, you know."

She laughed at that. "Okay. I'll come decently dressed. Saturday it is." She hesitated. "Where's the ranch?"

"I'll come and get you." He hesitated. "You'll still be here next Saturday, won't you?"

She was wondering how to stretch her investigation here by another week. Then she remembered that Christmas was Thursday and she relaxed. "I get Christmas off," she said. Then she remembered that she'd promised to work Christmas Eve already. "Well, I get Christmas Day. I'll ask for the rest of the week. I'll tell them that the case is heating up and I have two or three more people to interview."

"Great! Can I help?"

"Yes, you can find me two or three more people to interview," she said. "Meanwhile, I'll call Dolores and ask her to give me her minister's name." She grimaced. "I'll have to be sure I don't say that to whoever answers the phone. We told everybody we were giving her a message from her minister!"

"Good idea. Let me know what you find out, okay?"

"You bet. See you." She hung up.

She had to dial information to get the senator's number and, thank God, it wasn't unlisted. She punched the numbers into her cell phone and waited. A young woman answered.

"May I please speak to Dolores?" Alice asked politely.

"Dolores?"

"Yes."

There was a long pause. Alice gritted her teeth. They were going to tell her that employees weren't allowed personal phone calls during the day, she just knew it.

But the voice came back on the line with a long sigh. "I'm so sorry," the woman said. "Dolores isn't here anymore."

That wasn't altogether surprising, but it wasn't a serious setback. "Can you tell me how to get in touch with her? I'm an old friend," she added, improvising.

The sigh was longer. "Well, you can't. I mean, she's dead."

Alice was staggered. "Dead?!" she exclaimed.

"Yes. Suicide. She shot herself through the heart," the woman said sadly. "It was such a shock. The senator's wife found her... Oh, dear, I can't talk anymore, I'm sorry."

"Just a minute, just one minute, can you tell me where the funeral is being held?" she asked quickly.

"At the Weston Street Baptist Church," came the reply, almost in a whisper, "at two tomorrow afternoon. I have to go. I'm very sorry about Dolores. We all liked her."

The phone went dead.

Alice felt sick. Suicide! Had she driven the poor woman to it, with her questions? Or had she been depressed because of her boyfriend's murder?

Strange, that she'd shot herself through the heart. Most women chose some less violent way to die. Most used drugs. Suicides by gun were usually men.

She called Harley back.

"Hello?" he said.

"Harley, she killed herself," she blurted out.

"Who? Dolores? She's dead?" he exclaimed.

"Yes. Shot through the heart, I was told. Suicide."

He paused. "Isn't that unusual for a woman? To use a gun to kill herself, I mean?"

"It is. But I found out where her pastor is," she added. "I'm going to the funeral tomorrow. Right now, I'm going up to San Antonio to my office."

"Why?" he asked.

"Because in all violent deaths, even those ascribed to suicide, an autopsy is required. I wouldn't miss this one for the world."

"Keep in touch."

"You bet."

Alice hung up and went back to her van. She had a hunch that a woman as religious as Dolores wouldn't kill herself. Most religions had edicts against it. That didn't stop people from doing it, of course, but Dolores didn't strike Alice as the suicidal sort. She was going to see if the autopsy revealed anything.

The office was, as usual on holidays, overworked. She found one of the assistant medical examiners poring over reports in his office.

He looked up as she entered. "Jones! Could I get you to come back and work for us in autopsy again if I bribed you? It's getting harder and harder to find people who don't mind hanging around with the dead."

She smiled. "Sorry, Murphy," she said. "I'm happier with investigative work these days. Listen, do you have a suicide back there? First name Dolores, worked for a senator...?"

"Yep. I did her myself, earlier this evening." He shook his head. "She had small hands and the gun was a .45 Colt ACP," he replied. "How she ever cocked the damned thing, much less killed herself with it, is going to be one of the great unsolved mysteries of life. Added to that, she had carpal tunnel in her right hand. She'd had surgery at least once. Weakens the muscle, you know. We'd already ascertained that she was right-handed because there was more muscle attachment there—usual on the dominant side."

"You're sure it was suicide?" she pressed.

He leaned back in his chair, eyeing her through thick corrective lenses. "There was a rim burn around the entrance wound," he said, referring to the heat and flare of the shot in close-contact wounds. "But the angle of entry was odd."

She jumped on that. "Odd, how?"

"Diagonal," he replied. He pulled out his digital camera, ran through the files and punched up one. He handed her the camera. "That's the wound, anterior view. Pull up the next shot and you'll see where it exited, posterior."

She inhaled. "Wow!"

"Interesting, isn't it? Most people who shoot themselves with an automatic handgun do it holding the barrel to the head or under the chin. This was angled downward. And as I said before, her hand was too weak to manage this sort of weapon. There's something else."

"What?" she asked, entranced.

"The gun was found still clenched in her left hand."

"So?"

"Remember what I said about the carpel tunnel? She was right-handed."

She cocked her head. "Going to write it up as suspected homicide?"

"You're joking, right? Know who she worked for?"

She sighed. "Yes. Senator Fowler."

"Would you write it up as a suspected homicide or would you try to keep your job?"

That was a sticky question. "But if she was murdered…"

"The 'if' is subjective. I'm not one of those TV forensic people," he reminded her. "I'm two years from retirement, and I'm not risking my pension on a possibility. She goes out as a suicide until I get absolute proof that it wasn't."

Alice knew when that would be. "Could you at least put 'probable suicide,' Murphy?" she persisted. "Just for me?"

He frowned. "Why? Alice, do you know something that I need to know?"

She didn't dare voice her suspicions. She had no proof. She managed a smile. "Humor me. It won't rattle any cages, and if something comes up down the line, you'll have covered your butt. Right?"

He searched her eyes for a moment and then smiled warmly. "Okay. I'll put probable. But if you dig up something, you tell me first, right?"

She grinned. "Right."

Her next move was to go to the Weston Street Baptist Church and speak to the minister, but she had to wait until the funeral to do it. If she saw the man alone, someone might see her and his life could be in danger. It might be already. She wasn't sure what to do.

She went to police headquarters and found Detective Rick Marquez sitting at his desk. The office was almost empty, but there he was, knee-deep in file folders.

She tapped on the door and walked in at the same time.

"Alice!" He got to his feet. "Nice to see you."

"Is it? Why?" she asked suspiciously.

He glanced at the file folders and winced. "Any reason to take a break is a good one. Not that I'm sorry to see you," he added.

"What are you doing?" she asked as she took a seat in front of the desk.

"Poring over cold cases," he said heavily. "My lieutenant said I could do it on my own time, as long as I didn't advertise why I was doing it."

"Why are you doing it?" she asked curiously.

"Your murder down in Jacobsville nudged a memory or two," he said. "There was a case similar to it, also unsolved. It involved a fourteen-year-old girl who was driving a car reported stolen. She was also unrecognizable, but several of her teeth were still in place. They identified her by dental records. No witnesses, no clues."

"How long ago was this?" she asked.

He shrugged. "About seven years," he said. "In fact, it happened some time before Kilraven's family was killed."

"Could there be a connection?" she wondered aloud.

"I don't know. I don't see how the death of a teenage girl ties in to the murder of a cop's family." He smiled. "Maybe it's just a coincidence." He put the files aside. "Why are you up here?"

"I came to check the results of an autopsy," she said. "The woman who worked for Senator Fowler supposedly killed herself, but the bullet was angled downward, her hand was too weak to have pulled the trigger and the weapon was found clutched in the wrong hand."

He blew out his breath in a rush. "Some suicide."

"My thoughts, exactly."

"Talk to me, Jones."

"She was involved with the murder victim in Jacobsville, remember?" she asked him. "She wouldn't tell me his name, she swore she didn't know it. But she gave me the alias he used—the one I called and gave you— and she said he'd spoken to the minister of her church. He told her there was an accident that caused a lot of other people to die. He had a guilty conscience and he wanted to tell what he knew."

Marquez's dark eyes pinned hers. "Isn't that interesting."

"Isn't it?"

"You going to talk to the minister?"

"I want to, but I'm afraid to be seen doing it," she told him. "His life may be in danger if he knows something. Whatever is going on, it's big, and it has ties to powerful people."

"The senator, maybe?" he wondered aloud.

"Maybe."

"When did you talk to her?"

"There was a fundraiser at the senator's house. Harley Fowler took me…" She hadn't connected the names before. Now she did. The senator's name was Fowler. Harley's name was Fowler. The senator had recognized Harley, had approached him, had talked to him in a soft tone…

"Harley *Fowler?*" Marquez emphasized, making the same connection she did. "Harley's family?"

"I don't know," she said. "He didn't say anything to me. But the senator acted really strangely. He seemed to recognize Harley. And when Harley took me to my apartment, he didn't wait until I got inside the door. That's not like him. He was distracted."

"He comes from wealth and power, and he's working cattle for Cy Parks," Marquez mused. "Now isn't that a curious thing?"

"It is, and if it's true, you mustn't tell anybody," Alice replied. "It's his business."

"I agree. I'll keep it to myself. Who saw you talk to the woman at the senator's house?"

"Everybody, but we told them we knew her minister and came to tell her something for him."

"If she went to church every week, wouldn't that seem suspicious that you were seeing her to give her a message from her minister?"

Alice smiled. "Harley told them he'd asked us to give her a message about offering a ride to a fellow worshipper on Sunday."

"Uh, Alice, her car was pulled out of the Little Carmichael River in Jacobsville…?"

"Oh, good grief," she groaned. "Well, nobody knew that when we were at the party."

"Yes. But maybe somebody recognized you and figured you were investigating the murder," he returned.

She grimaced. "And I got her killed," she said miserably.

"No."

"If I hadn't gone there and talked to her…!" she protested.

"When your time's up, it's up, Jones," he replied philosophically. "It wouldn't have made any difference. A car crash, a heart attack, a fall from a high place…it could have been anything. Intentions are what matter. You didn't go there to cause her any trouble."

She managed a wan smile. "Thanks, Marquez."

"But if she was killed," he continued, "that fits into your case somehow. It means that the murderer isn't taking any chance that somebody might talk."

"The murderer…?"

"Your dead woman said the victim knew something damaging about several deaths. Who else but the murderer would be so hell-bent on eliminating evidence?"

"We still don't know who the victim is."

Marquez's sensuous lips flattened as he considered the possibilities. "If the minister knows anything, he's already in trouble. He may be in trouble if he doesn't know anything. The perp isn't taking any chances."

"What can we do to protect him?"

Marquez picked up the phone. "I'm going to risk my professional career and see if I can help him."

Alice sat and listened while he talked. Five minutes later, he hung up the phone.

"Are you sure that's the only way to protect him?" she asked worriedly.

"It's the best one I can think of, short of putting him in protective custody," he said solemnly. "I can't do that without probable cause, not to mention that our budget is in the red and we can't afford protective custody."

"Your boss isn't going to like it. And I expect Jon Blackhawk will be over here with a shotgun tomorrow morning, first thing."

"More than likely."

She smiled. "You're a prince!"

His eyebrows arched. "You could marry me," he suggested.

She shook her head. "No chance. If you really are a prince, if I kissed you, by the way the laws of probability work in my life, you'd turn right into a frog."

He hesitated and then burst out laughing.

She grinned. "Thanks, Marquez. If I can help you, anytime, I will."

"You can. Call my boss tomorrow and tell him that you think I'm suffering from a high fever and hallucinations and I'm not responsible for my own actions."

"I'll do that very thing. Honest."

The next morning, the local media reported that the pastor of a young woman who'd committed suicide was being questioned by police about some information that might tie her to a cold case. Alice thought it was a stroke of pure genius. Only a total fool would risk killing the pastor now that he was in the media spotlight. It was the best protection he could have.

Marquez's boss was, predictably, enraged. But Alice went to see him and, behind closed doors, told him what she knew about the murder in Jacobsville. He calmed down and agreed that it was a good call on his detective's part.

Then Alice went to see Reverend Mike Colman, early in the morning, before the funeral.

He wasn't what she expected. He was sitting in his office wearing sneakers, a pair of old jeans and a black sweatshirt. He had prematurely thinning dark hair, wore glasses, and had a smile as warm as a summer day.

He got up and shook hands with Alice after she introduced herself.

"I understand that I might be a candidate for admittance to your facility," he deadpanned. "Detective Marquez decided that making a media pastry out of me could save my life."

"I hope he's right," she said solemnly. "Two people have died in the past two weeks who had ties to this case. We've got a victim in Jacobsville that we can't even identify."

He grimaced. "I was sorry to hear about Dolores. I never thought she'd kill herself, and I still don't."

"It's sad that she did so much to help a man tortured by his past, and paid for it with her life. Isn't there a saying, that no good deed goes unpunished?" she added with wan humor.

"It seems that way sometimes, doesn't it?" he asked with a smile. "But God's ways are mysterious. We aren't meant to know why things happen the way they do at all times. So what can I do to help you?"

"Do you think you could describe the man Dolores sent to talk to you? If I get a police artist over here with his software and his laptop, can you tell him what the man looked like?"

"Oh, I think I can do better than that."

He pulled a pencil out of his desk drawer, drew a thick pad of paper toward him, peeled back the top and proceeded with deft strokes to draw an unbelievably lifelike pencil portrait of a man.

"That's incredible!" Alice exclaimed, fascinated by the expert rendering.

He chuckled as he handed it over to her. "Thanks. I wasn't always a minister," he explained. "I was on my way to Paris to further my studies in art when God tapped me on the shoulder and told me He needed me." He shrugged. "You don't say no to Him," he added with a kind smile.

"If there isn't some sort of pastor/confessor bond you'd be breaking, could you tell me what you talked about with him?"

"There's no confidentiality," he replied. "But he didn't really tell me anything. He asked me if God could forgive any sin, and I told him yes. He said he'd been a bad man, but he was in love, and he wanted to change. He said he was going to talk to somebody who was involved in an old case, and he'd tell me everything when he got back." He grimaced. "Except he didn't get back, did he?"

"No," Alice agreed sadly. "He didn't."

Seven

Alice took the drawing with her. She phoned Marquez's office, planning to stop by to show the drawing to him, but he'd already gone home. She tucked it into her purse and went to her own office. It was now Christmas Eve, and she'd promised to work tonight as a favor to the woman who'd saved her date with Harley.

She walked into the medical examiner's office, waving to the security guard on her way inside. The building, located on the University of Texas campus, was almost deserted. Only a skeleton crew worked on holidays. Most of the staff had families. Only Alice and one other employee were still single. But the medical examiner's office was accessible 24/7, so someone was always on call.

She went by her colleague's desk and grimaced as she saw the caseload sitting in the basket, waiting for her. It was going to be a long night.

She sat down at her own desk and started poring over the first case file. There were always deaths to investigate, even when foul play wasn't involved. In each one, if there was an question as to how the deceased had departed, it was up to her to work with the detectives to determine a cause of death. Her only consolation was that the police detectives were every bit as overloaded as she, a medical examiner investigator, was. Nobody did investigative work to get rich. But the job did have other rewards, she reminded herself. Solving a crime and bringing a murderer to justice was one of the perks. And no amount of money would make up for the pleasure it gave her to see that a death was avenged. Legally, of course.

She opened the first file and started working up the notes on the computer into a document easily read by the lead police detective on the case, as well as the assistant district attorney prosecuting it. She waded through crime scene photographs, measurements, witness statements and other interviews, but as she did, she was still wondering about the coincidence of Harley's last name and the senator's. The older man had recognized him, had called him Harley. They obviously knew each other, and there was some animosity there. But if the senator was a relation, why hadn't Harley mentioned it when he and Alice stopped by the house for the fundraiser?

Maybe he hadn't wanted Alice to know. Maybe he didn't want anyone to know, especially anyone in Jacobsville. Perhaps he wanted to make it on his own, without the wealth and power of his family behind him. He'd said that he no longer felt comfortable with the things his parents wanted him to do. If they were in politics and expected him to help host fundraisers and hang out with the cream of high society, he might have felt uncomfortable. She recalled her own parents and how much she'd loved them, and how close they'd been. They'd never asked her to do anything she didn't feel comfortable with. Harley obviously hadn't had that sort of home life. She was sad for him. But if things worked out, she promised herself that she'd do what she could to make up for what he missed. First step in that direction, she decided, was a special Christmas present.

She slept late on Christmas morning. But when she woke up, she got out her cell phone and made a virtual shopping trip around town, to discover which businesses were open on a holiday. She found one, and it carried just the item she wanted. She drove by there on her way down to Jacobsville.

Good thing she'd called ahead about keeping her motel room, she thought when she drove into the parking lot. The place was full. Obviously some locals had out-of-town family who didn't want to impose when they came visiting on the holidays. She stashed her suitcase and called Harley's number.

"Hello," came a disgruntled voice over the line.

"Harley?" she asked hesitantly.

There was a shocked pause. "Alice? Is that you?"

She laughed. "Well, you sound out of sorts."

"I am." There was a splash. "Get out of there, you walking steak platter!" he yelled. "Hold the line a minute, Alice, I have to put down the damn…phone!"

There was a string of very unpleasant language, most of which was mercifully muffled. Finally Harley came back on the line.

"I hate the cattle business," he said.

She grimaced. Perhaps she shouldn't have made that shopping trip after all. "Do you?" she asked. "Why?"

"Truck broke down in the middle of the pasture while I was tossing out hay," he muttered. "I got out of the truck and under the hood to see what was wrong. I left the door open. Boss's wife had sent me by the store on the way to pick up some turnip greens for her. Damned cow stuck her head into the truck and ate every damned one of them! So now, I'm mired up to my knees in mud and the truck's sinking, and once I get the truck out, I've got to go all the way back to town for a bunch of turnips on account of the stupid cow... Why are you laughing?"

"I thought you ran purebred bulls," she said.

"You can't get a purebred bull without a purebred cow to drop it," he said with exaggerated patience.

"Sorry. I wasn't thinking. Say, I'm just across the street from a market. Want me to go over and get you some more turnips and bring them to you?"

There was an intake of breath. "You'd do that? On Christmas Day?"

"I sort of got you something," she said. "Just a little something. I wanted an excuse to bring it to you, anyway."

"Doggone it, Alice, I didn't get you anything," he said shamefully.

"I didn't expect you to," she said at once. "But you took me to a nice party and I thought... Well, it's just a little something."

"I took you to a social shooting gallery and didn't even buy you supper," he said, feeling ashamed.

"It was a nice party," she said. "Do you want turnips or not?"

He laughed. "I do. Think you can find Cy Parks's ranch?"

"Give me directions."

He did, routing her the quickest way.

"I'll be there in thirty minutes," she said. "Or I'll call for more directions."

"Okay. Thanks a million, Alice."

"No problem."

She dressed in her working clothes, jeans and boots and a coat, but she added a pretty white sweater with a pink poinsettia embroidered on it, for Christmas. She didn't bother with makeup. It wouldn't help much anyway, she decided with a rueful smile. She bought the turnips and drove the few miles to the turnoff that led to Cy Parks's purebred Santa Gertrudis stud ranch.

Harley was waiting for her less than half a mile down the road, at the fork that turned into the ranch house. He was covered in mud, even his once-brown cowboy hat. He had a smear of mud on one cheek, but he looked very sexy, Alice thought. She couldn't think of one man out of thirty she knew who could be covered in mud and still look so good. Harley did.

He pushed back his hat as he walked up to the van, opening the door for her.

She grabbed the turnips in their brown bag and handed it to him. She jumped down with a small box in her hand. "Here," she said, shoving it at him.

"Wait a sec." He put the turnips in his truck and handed her a five-dollar bill. "Don't argue," he said at once, when she tried to. "I had money to get them with, even allowing for cow sabotage." He grinned.

She grinned back. "Okay." She put the bill in her slacks pocket and handed him the box.

He gave her an odd look. "What's it for?"

"Christmas," she said.

He laughed. "Boss gives me a bonus every Christmas. I can't remember the last time I got an actual present."

She flushed.

"Don't get self-conscious about it," he said, when he noticed her sudden color. "I just felt bad that I didn't get you something."

"I told you, the party…"

"Some party," he muttered. He turned the small box in his hands, curious. He pulled the tape that held the sides together and opened it. His pale eyes lit up as he pulled the little silver longhorn tie tack out of the box. "Hey, this is sweet! I've been looking for one of these, but I could never find one small enough to be in good taste!"

She flushed again. "You really like it?"

"I do! I'll wear it to the next Cattlemen's Association meeting," he promised. "Thanks, Alice."

"Merry Christmas."

"It is, now," he agreed. He slid an arm around her waist and pulled her against him. "Merry Christmas, Alice." He bent and kissed her with rough affection.

She sighed and melted into him. The kiss was warm, and hard and intoxicating. She was a normal adult woman with all the usual longings, but it had been a long time since a kiss had made her want to rip a man's clothes off and push him down on the ground.

She laughed.

He drew back at once, angry. "What the hell…!"

"No, it's not… I'm not laughing at you! I was wondering what you'd think if I started ripping your clothes off…!"

He'd gone from surprise to anger to indignation, and now he doubled over laughing.

"Was it something I said?" she wondered aloud.

He grabbed her up in his arms and spun her around, catching her close to kiss her hungrily again and again. He was covered in mud, and now she was covered in it, too. She didn't care.

Her arms caught around his neck. She held on, loving the warm crush of his mouth in the cold rain that was just starting to fall. Her eyes closed. She breathed, and breathed him, cologne and soap and coffee…

After a few seconds, the kiss stopped being fun and became serious. His hard mouth opened. His arm dragged her breasts against his broad chest. He nudged her lips apart and invaded her mouth with deliberate sensuality.

He nibbled her lower lip as he carried her to the pickup truck. He nudged the turnips into the passenger seat while he edged under the wheel, still carrying Alice. He settled her in his lap and kissed her harder while his hands slid under the warm sweater and onto her bare back, working their way under the wispy little bra she was wearing.

His hands were cold and she jumped when they found her pert little breasts, and she laughed nervously.

"They'll warm up," he whispered against her mouth.

She was going under in waves of pleasure. It had been such a long time since she'd been held and kissed, and even the best she'd had was nothing compared to this. She moaned softly as his palms settled over her breasts and began to caress them, ever so gently.

She held on for dear life. She hoped he wasn't going

to suggest that they try to manage an intimate session on the seat, because there really wasn't that much room. On the other hand, she wasn't protesting…

When he drew back, she barely realized it. She was hanging in space, so flushed with delight that she was feeling oblivious to everything else.

He was looking at her with open curiosity, his hands still under her top, but resting on her rib cage now, not intimately on her breasts.

She blinked, staring up at him helplessly. "Is something wrong?" she asked in a voice that sounded drowsy with passion.

"Alice, you haven't done much of this, have you?" he asked very seriously.

She bit her lip self-consciously. "Am I doing it wrong?"

"There's no right or wrong way," he corrected gently. "You don't know how to give it back."

She just stared at him.

"It's not a complaint," he said when he realized he was hurting her feelings. He bent and brushed his warm mouth over her eyelids. "For a brash woman, you're amazingly innocent. I thought you were kidding, about being a virgin."

She went scarlet. "Well, no, I wasn't."

He laughed softly. "I noticed. Here. Sit up."

She did, but she popped back up and grabbed the turnips before she sat on them. "Whew," she whistled. "They're okay."

He took them from her and put them up on the dash.

She gave him a mock hurt look. "Don't you want to ravish me on the truck seat?" she asked hopefully.

He lifted both eyebrows. "Alice, you hussy!" He laughed.

She grimaced. "Sorry."

"I was teasing!"

"Oh."

He drew her close and hugged her with rough affection. "Yes, I'd love to ravish you on the seat, but not on Christmas Day in plain view of the boss and any cowhand who wandered by."

"Are they likely to wander by?" she wondered out loud.

He let her go and nodded in the direction of the house. There were two cowboys coming their way on horseback. They weren't looking at them. They seemed to be talking.

"It's Christmas," she said.

"Yes, and cattle have to be worked on holidays as well as workdays," he reminded her.

"Sorry. I forgot."

"I really like my tie tack," he said. "And thanks a million for bringing me the turnips." He hesitated. "But I have to get back to work. I gave up my day off so that John could go and see his kids," he added with a smile.

She beamed. "I gave up my Christmas Eve for the same reason. But that's how I got to go to the party with you. I promised to work for him last night."

"We're both nice people," he said, smiling.

She sighed. "I could call a minister right now."

"He's busy," he said with a grin. "It's Christmas."

"Oh. Right."

He got out of the truck and helped her down. "Thanks for my present. Sorry I didn't get you one."

"Yes, you did," she said at once, and then laughed and flushed.

He bent and kissed her softly. "I got an extra one myself," he whispered. "Are we still going riding Saturday?"

"Oh, yes," she said. "At least, I think so. I've got to run up to San Antonio in the morning to talk to Rick Marquez. The minister of the murdered woman was able to draw the man she sent to him."

"Really?" he asked, impressed.

"Yes, and so now we have a real lead." She frowned thoughtfully. "You know, I wonder if Kilraven might recognize the guy. He works out of San Antonio. He might make a copy and show it to his brother, too."

"Good idea." He drew in a long breath. "Alice, you be careful," he added. "If the woman was killed because she talked to us, the minister might be next, and then you." He didn't add, but they both knew, that he could be on the firing line, too.

"The minister's okay. Marquez called a reporter he knew and got him on the evening news." She chuckled. "They'd be nuts to hurt him now, with all the media attention."

"Probably true, and good call by Marquez. But you're not on the news."

"Point taken. I'll watch my back. You watch yours, too," she added with a little concern.

"I work for a former mercenary," he reminded her drolly. "It would take somebody really off balance to come gunning for me."

"Okay. That makes me feel better." She smiled. "But if this case heats up in San Antonio, I may have to go back sooner than Saturday…"

"So? If you can't come riding, I can drive up there and we can catch a movie or go out to eat."

"You would?" she exclaimed, surprised.

He glowered at her. "We're going steady. Didn't you notice?"

"No! Why didn't you tell me?" she demanded.

"You didn't ask. Go back to the motel and maybe we can have lunch tomorrow at Barbara's. I'll phone you."

She grinned. "That would be lovely."

"Meanwhile, I've got more cattle to feed," he said on a weary sigh. "It was a nice break, though."

"Yes, it was."

He looked at the smears of mud on her once-pristine shirt and winced. "Sorry," he said.

She looked down at the smears and just laughed. "It'll wash," she said with a shy smile.

He beamed. He loved a woman who didn't mind a little dirt. He opened her van door and she climbed up into it. "Drive carefully," he told her.

She smiled. "I always do."

"See you."

"See you."

She was halfway back to the motel before she realized that she hadn't mentioned his connection to Senator Fowler. Of course, that might be just as well, considering that the newest murder victim had ties to the senator, and the original murder victim did, too, in a roundabout way.

On her way to see Hayes Carson at the sheriff's office, Alice phoned Marquez at home—well, it was a holiday, so she thought he might be at home with his foster mother, Barbara. She found out that Marquez had been called back to San Antonio on a case. She grimaced. She was never going to get in touch with him, she supposed.

She walked into Carson's office. He was sitting at his desk. He lifted both eyebrows. "It's December twenty-fifth," he pointed out.

She lifted both eyebrows. "Ho, ho, ho?" she said.

He chuckled. "So I'm not the only person who works holidays. I had started to wonder." He indicated the empty desks around his office in the county detention center.

"My office looked that way last night, too," she confessed. She sat down by his desk. "I questioned a woman who worked for Senator Fowler about the man who drove her car down here and got killed next to the river."

"Find out much?" he asked, suddenly serious.

"That I shouldn't have been so obvious about questioning her. She died of an apparent suicide, but I pestered the attending pathologist to put 'probable' before 'suicide' on the death certificate. She shot herself through the heart with the wrong hand and the bullet was angled down." She waited for a reaction.

He leaned back in his chair. "Wonders will never cease."

"I went to see her minister, who spoke to the man we found dead by the river. The minister was an art student. He drew me this." She pulled out a folded sheet of paper from her purse and handed it to him.

"Hallelujah!" he burst out. "Alice, you're a wonder! You should be promoted!"

"No, thanks, I like fieldwork too much," she told him, grinning. "It's good, isn't it? That's what your murder victim looks like." Her smile faded. "I'm just sorry I got the woman killed who was trying to help him restart his life."

He looked up with piercing eyes. "You didn't. Life happens. We don't control how it happens."

"You're good for my self-esteem. I was going to show that to Rick Marquez, but he's become rather elusive."

"Something happened in San Antonio. I don't know what. They called in a lot of off-duty people."

"Was Kilraven one of them, or do you know?" she asked.

"I don't, but I can find out." He called the dispatch center and gave Kilraven's badge number and asked if Kilraven was on duty.

"Yes, he is. Do you want me to ask him to place you a twenty-one?" she asked, referring to a phone call.

"Yes, thanks, Winnie," he said, a smile in his voice as he recognized dispatcher Winnie Sinclair.

"No problem. Dispatch out at thirteen hundred hours."

He hung up. "She'll have him call me," he told Alice. "What did the minister tell you about the murdered man?" he asked while they waited.

"Not much. He said the guy told him he'd been a bad man, but he wanted to change, that he was going to speak to somebody about an old case and that he'd talk to the minister again after he did it. It's a real shame. Apparently he'd just discovered that there was more to life than dodging the law. He had a good woman friend, he was starting to go to church—now he's lying in the morgue, unidentifiable."

"Not anymore," Hayes told her, waving the drawing.

"Yes, but he could be anybody," she replied.

"If he has a criminal background, he's got finger-prints on file and a mug shot. I have access to face recognition software."

"You do? How?" she asked, fascinated.

"Tell you what," he said, leaning forward. "I'll give you my source if you'll tell me how you got hold of that computer chip emplacement tech for tagging bodies."

She caught her breath. "Well! You do get around, don't you? That's cutting-edge and we don't advertise it."

"My source doesn't advertise, either."

"We'll trade," she promised. "Now, tell me…"

The phone rang. Hayes picked it up. He gave Alice a sardonic look. "Yes, the sheriff's office is open on Christmas. I just put away my reindeer and took off my red suit… Yes, Alice Jones is here with an artist's sketch of the murdered man… Hello? Hello?" He hung up with a sigh. "Kilraven," he said, answering the unasked question.

Alice sighed. "I get that a lot, too. People hanging up on me, I mean. I'll bet he's burning rubber, trying to get here at light speed."

"I wouldn't doubt it." He chuckled.

Sure enough, just a minute or two later, they heard squealing tires turning into the parking lot outside the window. A squad car with flashing blue lights slammed to a stop just at the front door and the engine went dead. Seconds later, Kilraven stormed into the office.

"Let's see it," he said without preamble.

Hayes handed him the drawing.

Kilraven looked at it for a long time, frowning.

"Recognize him?" Alice asked.

He grimaced. "No," he said gruffly. "Damn! I thought it might be somebody I knew."

"Why?" Hayes asked.

"I work out of San Antonio as a rule," he said. "And I was a patrol officer, and then a detective, on the police force there for some years. If the guy had a record in San Antonio, I might have had dealings with him. But I don't recognize this guy."

Hayes took the sketch back. "If I make a copy, could you show it to Jon and see if he looks familiar to him?"

"Sure." He glanced at Alice. "How'd you get a sketch of the dead man? Reconstructive artist?"

"No. That woman I talked to about him killed herself…"

"Like hell she did," Kilraven exclaimed. "That's too pat!"

"Just what I thought. I talked to the forensic pathologist who did the autopsy," she added. "He said she was right-handed, but shot herself through the heart with her left hand. Good trick, too, because she had carpal tunnel syndrome, plus surgery, and the gun was a big, heavy .45 Colt ACP. He said she'd have had hell just cocking it."

"He labeled it a suicide?"

She shook her head. "He's trying not to get caught up in political fallout. She worked for the senator, you know, and he's not going to want to be a media snack over a possible homicide that happened on his own property."

"The pathologist didn't label it a suicide?" he persisted.

"I got him to add 'probable' to the report."

"Well, that's something, I guess. Damned shame, about the woman. She might have been able to tell us more, in time." He smiled at Alice. "I'm glad you went to see her, anyway. What we have is thanks to you." He frowned. "But how did you get the sketch?"

"The woman's minister," she said simply. "He'd talked to the man who was killed and before he became a minister, he was an artist. He didn't add much to what the woman had already told me. He did say that the guy had a guilty conscience and he was going to talk to somebody about an old case."

Kilraven was frowning again. "An old case. Who was he going to talk to? People in law enforcement, maybe?"

"Very possibly," Alice agreed. "I'm not through digging. But I need to identify this man. I thought I might go to the motel where he was staying and start interviewing residents. It's a start."

"Not for you," Kilraven said sternly. "You've put yourself in enough danger already. You leave this to me and Jon. We get paid for people to shoot at us. You don't."

"My hero," Alice sighed, batting her eyelashes at him and smiling. "If I wasn't so keen to marry Harley Fowler, I swear I'd be sending you candy and flowers."

"I hate sweets and I'm allergic to flowers," he pointed out.

She wrinkled her nose. "Just as well, then, isn't it?"

"I'll copy this for you," Hayes said, moving to the copy machine in the corner. "We're low on toner, though, so don't expect anything as good as the original drawing."

"Why don't you get more toner?" Alice asked.

Hayes glowered. "I have to have a purchase order from the county commission, and they're still yelling at me about the last several I asked for."

"Which was for…?" Kilraven prompted.

Hayes made the copy, examined it and handed it to Kilraven. "A cat, and an electrician, and an exterminator."

Alice and Kilraven stared at him.

He moved self-consciously back to his desk and sat down. "I bought this cheap cat," he emphasized. "It only cost fifteen bucks at the pet store. It wasn't pure-bred or anything."

"Why did you buy a cat?" Alice asked.

He sighed. "Do you remember the mouse that lived in Tira Hart's house before she became Simon Hart's wife?"

"Well, I heard about it," Kilraven admitted.

"One of my deputies caught two field mice and was going to take them home to his kids for a science project. He put them in a wood box and when he went to get them out, they weren't there." Hayes sighed. "They chewed their way out of the box, they chewed up the baseboards and two electrical wires, and did about three hundred dollars worth of damage to county property. I called an electrician for that. Then I tried traps and they wouldn't work, so I bought a cat."

"Did the cat get the mice?" Alice asked.

Hayes shook his head. "Actually," he replied, "the mice lay in wait for the cat, chomped down on both his paws at the same time, and darted back into the hole in the wall they came out of. Last time I saw the cat, he was headed out of town by way of the city park. The mice are still here, though," he added philosophically. "Which is why I had to have authorization to pay for an exterminator. The chairman of our county commission found one of the mice sitting in his coffee cup." He sighed. "Would you believe, I got blamed for that, too?"

"Well, that explains why the commission got mad at you," Alice said. "I mean, for the cat and the electrician."

"No, that's not why they got mad."

"It wasn't?"

He looked sheepish. "It was the engine for a 1996 Ford pickup truck."

Alice stared at him. "Okay, now I'm confused."

"I had to call an exterminator. While he was looking for the mice, they got under the hood of his truck and did something—God knows what, but it was catastrophic. When he started the truck, the engine caught fire. It was a total loss."

"How do you know the mice did it?" Kilraven wanted to know.

"One of my deputies—the same one who brought the damned rodents in here in the first place—saw them coming down the wheel well of the truck just before the exterminator got in and started it."

Alice laughed. She got to her feet. "Hayes, if I were you, I'd find whoever bought Cag Hart's big albino python and borrow him."

"If these mice are anything like Tira's mouse, fat chance a snake will do what a cat can't."

As he spoke, the lights started dimming. He shook his head. "They're back," he said with sad resignation.

"Better hide your firearms," Kilraven advised as he and Alice started for the door.

"With my luck, they're better shots than I am." Hayes laughed. "I'm going to show this drawing around town and see if anybody recognizes the subject. If either of you find out anything else about the murdered man, let me know."

"Will do," Alice promised.

Eight

Alice followed Kilraven out the door. He stood on the steps of the detention center, deep in thought.

"Why did you think you might know the murder victim?" Alice asked him.

"I told you…"

"You lied."

He looked down at her with arched eyebrows.

"Oh, I'm psychic," she said easily. "You know all those shows about people with ESP who solve murders, well, I get mistaken for that dishy one all the time…"

"You're not psychic, Alice," he said impatiently.

"No sense of humor," she scoffed. "I wonder how you stay sane on the job! Okay, okay—" she held up both hands when he glowered "—I'll talk. It was the way you rushed over here to look at the drawing. Come on, give me a break. Nobody gets in that sort of hurry without a pretty sturdy reason."

He rested his hand on the holstered butt of his pistol. His eyes held that "thousand-yard stare" that was so remarked on in combat stories. "I've encouraged a former San Antonio detective to do some digging into the files on my cold case," he said quietly. "And you aren't to mention that to Marquez. He's in enough trouble. We're not going to tell him."

She wouldn't have dared mention that she already knew about the detective working on the case, and so did Marquez. "Have you got a lead?" she asked.

"I thought this case might be one," he said quietly. "A guy comes down here from San Antonio, and gets killed. It's eerie, but I had a feeling that he might have been looking for me. Stupid, I know…"

"There are dozens of reasons he might have driven down here," she replied. "And he might have been passing through. The perp might have followed him and ambushed him."

"You're right, of course." He managed a smile. "I keep hoping I'll get lucky one day." The smile faded into cold steel. "I want to know who it was. I want to make him pay for the past seven miserable years of my life."

She cocked her head, frowning. "Nothing will make up for that," she said quietly. "You can't take two lives out of someone. There's no punishment on earth that will take away the pain, or the loss. You know that."

"Consciously, I do," he said. He drew in a sharp breath. "I worked somebody else's shift as a favor that night. If I hadn't, I'd have been with them…"

"Stop that!" she said in a tone short enough to shock him. "Lives have been destroyed with that one, stupid word. *If!* Listen to me, Kilraven, you can't appropriate the power of life and death. You can't control the world. Sometimes people die in horrible ways. It's not right, but it's just the way things are. You have to go forward. Living in regret is only another way the perp scores off you."

He didn't seem to take offense. He was actually listening.

"I hear it from victims' families all the time," she continued. "They grieve, they hate, they live for vengeance. They can't wait for the case to go to trial so they can watch the guilty person burn. But, guess what, juries don't convict, or perps make deals, or sometimes the case even gets thrown out of court because of a break in the chain of evidence. And all that anger has no place to go, except in sound bites for the six-o'clock news. Then the families go home and the hatred grows, and they end up with empty lives full of nothing. Nothing at all. Hate takes the place that healing should occupy."

He stared down at her for a long moment. "I guess I've been there."

"For about seven years," she guessed. "Are you going to devote your life to all that hatred? You'll grow old with nothing to show for those wasted years except bitter memories."

"If my daughter had lived," he said in a harsh tone, "she'd be ten years old next week."

She didn't know how to answer him. The anguish he felt was in every word.

"He got away with it, Jones," he said harshly.

"No, he didn't," she replied. "Someone knows what happened, and who did it. One day, a telephone will ring in a detective's office, and a jilted girlfriend or boyfriend will give up the perp out of hurt or revenge or greed."

He relaxed a little. "You really think so?"

"I've seen it happen. So have you."

"I guess I have."

"Try to stop living in the past," she counseled gently. "It's a waste of a good man."

He lifted an eyebrow, and the black mood seemed to drop away. His silver eyes twinkled. "Flirting with me?"

"Don't go there," she warned. "I've seen too many wives sitting up watching the late show, hoping their husbands would come home. That's not going to be me. I'm going to marry a cattle rancher and sleep nights."

He grinned. "That's no guarantee of sleep. Baby bulls and cows almost always get born in the wee hours of the morning."

"You'd know," she agreed, smiling. "You and Jon have that huge black Angus ranch in Oklahoma, don't you?"

He nodded. "Pity neither of us wants to sit around and babysit cattle. We're too career conscious."

"When you get older, it might appeal."

"It might," he said, but not with any enthusiasm. "We hold on to it because Jon's mother likes to have company there." He grimaced. "She's got a new prospect for Jon."

"I heard." Alice chuckled. "He had her arrested in his own office for sexual harassment. I understand Joceline Perry is still making him suffer for it."

"It really was sexual harassment," Kilraven corrected. "The woman is a call girl. We both tried to tell my stepmom, but her best friend is the woman's mother. She won't believe us. Mom keeps trying to get her to the ranch, with the idea that Jon will like her better if he sees her in blue jeans."

"Fat chance," Alice said. "Jon should tell Joceline the truth."

"He won't lower his dignity that far. He said if she wants to think he's that much of a scoundrel, let her. They don't get along, anyway."

"No offense, but most women don't get along with your brother," she replied. "He doesn't really like women very much."

He sighed. "If you had my stepmother as a mom, you wouldn't, either." He held up a hand. "She has her good qualities. But she has blind spots and prejudices that would choke a mule. God help the woman who really falls in love with Jon. She'll have to get past Jon's mother, and it will take a tank."

She pursed her lips. "I hear Joceline has the personality of a tank."

He chuckled. "She does. But she hates Jon." He hesitated. "If you get any new leads, you'll tell me, right?"

"Right."

"Thanks for the lecture," he added with twinkling eyes. "You're not bad."

"I'm terrific," she corrected. "Just you wait. Harley Fowler will be rushing me to the nearest minister any day now."

"Poor guy."

"Hey, you stop that. I'm a catch, I am. I've got movie stars standing in line trying to marry me... Where are you going?"

"Back to work while there's still time," he called over his shoulder.

Before she could add to her bragging, he hopped into his squad car and peeled out of the parking lot.

Alice stared after him. "You'd be lucky if I set my sights on you," she said to nobody in particular. "It's your loss!" she called after the retreating squad car.

A deputy she hadn't heard came up behind her. "Talking to yourself again, Jones?" he mused.

She gave him a pained glance. "It's just as well that I do. I'm not having much luck getting people to listen to me."

"I know just how that feels," he said with a chuckle.

He probably did, she thought as she went back to her van. People in law enforcement were as much social workers as law enforcers. They had to be diplomatic, keep their tempers under extraordinary provocation, hand out helpful advice and firm warnings, sort out domestic problems, handle unruly suspects and even dodge bullets.

Alice knew she was not cut out for that sort of life, but she enjoyed her job. At least, she chuckled, she didn't have to dodge bullets.

Saturday, she was still in Jacobsville, waiting for one last piece of evidence that came from the site of the car that was submerged in the river. A fisherman had found a strange object near the site and called police. Hayes Carson had driven out himself to have a look. It was a metal thermos jug that the fisherman had found in some weeds. It looked new and still had liquid in it. Could have been that some other pedestrian lost it, Hayes confided, but it paid to keep your options open. Hayes had promised that Alice could have it, but she'd promised to go riding with Harley. So she'd told Hayes she'd pick it up at his office late that afternoon.

"And you think the sheriff himself sits at his desk waiting for people on a Saturday?" Hayes queried on the phone in mock horror.

"Listen, Hayes, I have it on good authority that you practically sleep at the office most nights and even keep

a razor and toothbrush there," she said with droll humor.
"So I'll see you about seven."

He sighed. "I'll be here, working up another
budget proposal."

"See?" She hung up.

Cy Parks wasn't what she'd expected. He was tall
and lean, with black hair showing just threads of gray,
and green eyes. His wife, Lisa, was shorter and blonde
with light eyes and glasses. They had two sons, one who
was a toddler and the other newborn. Lisa was holding
one, Cy had the oldest.

"We've heard a lot about you," Cy mused as Alice
stood next to Harley. They were all wearing jeans and
long-sleeved shirts and coats. It was a cold day.

"Most of it is probably true," Alice sighed. "But I
have great teeth—" she displayed them "—and a
good attitude."

They laughed.

"We haven't heard bad things," Lisa assured her,
adjusting her glasses on her pert nose.

"Yes, we have." Cy chuckled. "Not really bad ones.
Harley says you keep proposing to him, is all."

"Oh, that's true," Alice said, grinning. "I'm wearing
him down, day by day. I just can't get him to let me buy
him a ring."

Cy pursed his lips and glanced at Harley. "Hey, if you
can get him in a suit, I'll give him away," he promised.

Harley grinned at him. "I'll remind you that you said
that," he told his boss.

Cy's eyes were more kind than humorous. "I mean it."

Harley flushed a little with pleasure. "Thanks."

"Does that mean yes?" Alice asked Harley, wide-eyed.

He gave her a mock glare. "It means I'm thinking about it."

"Darn," she muttered.

"How's your murder investigation coming?" Cy asked suddenly.

"You mean the DB on the river?" she asked. "Slowly. We've got evidence. We just can't puzzle out what it means."

"There are some messed-up people involved, is my guess," Cy said, somber. "I've seen people handled the way your victim was. It usually meant a very personal grudge."

Alice nodded. "We've found that most close-up attacks, when they aren't random, are done by people with a grudge. I never cease to be amazed at what human beings are capable of."

"Amen." Cy slid an arm around Lisa. "We'd better get these boys back into a warm house. We've been through the mill with colds already." He chuckled. "Nice to meet you, Alice. If you can get him—" he pointed at Harley "—to marry you, I've already promised him some land and a seed herd of my best cattle."

"That's really nice of you," Alice said, and meant it.

Cy glanced at Harley warmly. "I'd kind of like to keep him close by," he said with a smile. "I'd miss him."

Harley seemed to grow two feet. "I'm not going anywhere," he drawled, but he couldn't hide that he was flattered.

"Come back again," Lisa told Alice. "It's hard to find two minutes to talk with little guys like these around—" she indicated her babies "—but we'll manage."

"I'd love to," Alice told her.

The Parks family waved and went into the house.

"They're nice," Alice said to Harley.

He nodded. "Mr. Parks has been more of a father to me than my own ever was."

Alice wanted to comment, to ask about the senator. But the look on Harley's face stopped her. It was traumatic. "I haven't been on a horse in about two years," she told him. "I had to go out with the Texas Rangers to look at some remains in the brush country, and it was the only way to get to the crime scene." She groaned. "Six hours on horseback, through prickly pear cactus and thorny bushes! My legs were scratched even through thick jeans and they felt like they were permanently bowed when I finally got back home."

"I've been there, too." He laughed. "But we won't go six hours, I promise."

He led her into the barn, where he already had two horses saddled. Hers was a pinto, a female, just the right size.

"That's Bean," he said. "Colby Lane's daughter rides her when she comes over here."

"Bean?" she asked as she mounted.

"She's a pinto," he said dryly.

She laughed. "Oh!"

He climbed into the saddle of a black Arabian gelding and led off down the trail that ran to the back of the property.

It was a nice day to go riding, she thought. It had rained the night before, but it was sunny today, if cold. There were small mud patches on the trail, and despite the dead grass and bare trees, it felt good to be out-of-doors on a horse.

She closed her eyes and smelled the clean scent of

country air. "If you could bottle this air," she commented, "you could outsell perfume companies."

He chuckled. "You sure could. It's great, isn't it? People in cities don't even know what they're missing."

"You lived in a city once, didn't you?" she asked in a conversational tone.

He turned his head sideways. Pale blue eyes narrowed under the wide brim of his hat as he pondered the question. "You've been making connections, Alice."

She flushed a little. "No, I really haven't. I've just noticed similarities."

"In names," he replied.

"Yes," she confessed.

He drew in a breath and drew in the reins. So did she. He sat beside her quietly, his eyes resting on the horizon.

"The senator is your father," she guessed.

He grimaced. "Yes."

She averted her gaze to the ground. It was just faintly muddy and the vegetation was brown. The trees in the distance were bare. It was a cold landscape. Cold, like Harley's expression.

"My parents were always in the middle of a cocktail party or a meeting. All my life. I grew up hearing the sound of ice clinking in glasses. We had politicians and other rich and famous people wandering in and out. I was marched out before bedtime to show everybody what a family man the politician was." He laughed coldly. "My mother was a superior court judge," he added surprisingly. "Very solemn on the bench, very strict at home. My sister died, and suddenly she was drinking more heavily than my father at those cocktail parties. She gave up her job on the bench to become an importer." He shook his head. "He changed, too. When he was younger, he'd play ball with me, or take me to the movies. After my sister died, everything was devoted to his career, to campaigning, even when he wasn't up for reelection. I can't tell you how sick I got of it."

"I can almost imagine," she said gently. "I'm sorry."

He turned back to her, frowning. "I never connected those two facts. You know, my sister's death with the changes in my parents. I was just a kid myself, not really old enough to think deeply." He glanced back at the horizon. "Maybe I was wrong."

"Maybe you were both wrong," she corrected. "Your father seemed very sad when he saw you."

"It's been almost eight years," he replied. "In all that time, not one card or phone call. It's hard to square that with any real regret."

"Sometimes people don't know how to reach out," she said. "I've seen families alienated for years, all because they didn't know how to make the first contact, take the first step back to a relationship that had gone wrong."

He sighed, fingering the bridle. "I guess that describes me pretty well."

"It's pride, isn't it?" she asked.

He laughed faintly. "Isn't it always?" he wondered aloud. "I felt that I was the wronged party. I didn't think it was up to me to make the first move. So I waited."

"Maybe your father felt the same way," she suggested.

"My father isn't the easiest man to approach, even on his good days," he said. "He has a temper."

"You weren't singing happy songs the day I called you, when the cow ate your turnips," she replied, tongue-in-cheek.

He laughed. "I guess I've got a temper, too."

"So do I. It isn't exactly a bad trait. Only if you carry it to extremes."

He looked down at his gloved hands. "I guess."

"They're not young people anymore, Harley," she said quietly. "If you wait too much longer, you may not get the chance to patch things up."

He nodded. "I've been thinking about that."

She hesitated. She didn't want to push too hard. She nudged her horse forward a little, so that she was even with him. "Have you thought about what sort of ring you'd like?"

He pursed his lips and glanced over at her. "One to go on my finger, or one to go through my nose?"

She laughed. "Stop that."

"Just kidding." He looked up. "It's getting cloudy. We'd better get a move on, or we may get caught in a rain shower."

She knew the warning was his way of ending the conversation. But she'd got him thinking. That was enough, for now. "Suits me."

He walked her back to the van, his hands in his pockets, his thoughts far away.

"I enjoyed today," she told him. "Thanks for the riding lesson."

He stopped at the driver's door of the van and looked down at her, a little oddly. "You don't push, do you?" he asked solemnly. "It's one of the things I like best about you."

"I don't like being pushed, myself," she confided. She searched his eyes. "You're a good man."

He drew his hand out of his pocket and smoothed back her windblown dark hair, where it blew onto her cheek. The soft leather of the glove tickled. "You're a good woman," he replied. "And I really mean that."

She started to speak.

He bent and covered her mouth with his before she could say anything. His lips parted, cold and hungry on her soft, pliable lips. She opened them with a sigh and reached around him with both arms, and held on tight. She loved kissing him. But it was more than affection. It was a white-hot fire of passion that made her ache from head to toe. She felt swollen, hot, burning, as his arms contracted.

"Oh, God," he groaned, shivering as he buried his mouth in her neck. "Alice, we're getting in too deep, too quick."

"Complaints, complaints," she grumbled into his coat.

He laughed despite the ache that was almost doubling him over. "It's not a complaint. Well, not exactly." He drew in a calming breath and slowly let her go. His eyes burned down into hers. "We can't rush this," he said. "It's too good. We have to go slow."

Her wide, dark blue eyes searched his languidly. She was still humming all over with pleasure. "Go slow." She nodded. Her eyes fell to his mouth.

"Are you hearing me?"

She nodded. Her gaze was riveted to the sensuous lines of his lips. "Hearing."

"Woman…!"

He caught her close again, ramming his mouth down onto hers. He backed her into the door of the van and ground his body against hers in a fever of need that echoed in her harsh moan.

For a long time, they strained together in the misting rain, neither capable of pulling back. Just when it seemed that the only way to go was into the back of the van, he managed to jerk his mouth back from hers and step away. His jaw was so taut, it felt as if his mouth might break. His pale blue eyes were blazing with frustrated need.

Her mouth was swollen and red. She leaned back against the door, struggling to breathe normally as she stared up at him with helpless adoration. He wasn't obviously muscular, but that close, she felt every taut line of his body. He was delicious, she thought. Like candy. Hard candy.

"You have to leave. Now." He said it in a very strained tone.

"Leave." She nodded again.

"Leave. Now."

She nodded. "Now."

"Alice," he groaned. "Honey, there are four pairs of eyes watching us out the window right now, and two pairs of them are getting a hell of a sex education!"

"Eyes." She blinked. "Eyes?"

She turned. There, in the living-room window, were four faces. The adult ones were obviously amused. The little ones were wide-eyed with curiosity.

Alice blushed. "Oh, dear."

"You have to go. Right now." He moved her gently aside and opened the door. He helped her up onto the seat. He groaned. "I'm not having supper in the big house tonight, I can promise you that," he added.

She began to recover her senses and her sense of humor. Her eyes twinkled. "Oh, I see," she mused. "I've compromised you. Well, don't you worry, sweetheart," she drawled. "I'll save your reputation. You can marry me tomorrow."

He laughed. "No. I'm trimming horses' hooves."

She glowered at him. "They have farriers to do that."

"Our farrier is on Christmas vacation," he assured her.

"One day," she told him, "you'll run out of excuses."

He searched her eyes and smiled softly. "Of course I will." He stepped back. "But not today. I'll phone you." He closed the door.

She started the engine and powered down the window. "Thanks for the ride."

He was still smiling. "Thanks for the advice. I'll take it."

"Merry Christmas."

He cocked his head. "Christmas is over."

"New Year's is coming."

"That reminds me, we have a New Year's celebration here," he said. "I can bring you to it."

"I'll be back in San Antonio then," she said miserably.

"I'll drive you down here and then drive you home."

"No. I'll stay in the motel," she said. "I don't want you on the roads after midnight. There are drunk drivers."

His heart lifted. His eyes warmed. "You really are a honey."

She smiled. "Hold that thought. See you."

He winked at her and chuckled when she blushed again. "See you, pretty girl."

She fumbled the van into gear and drove off jerkily. It had been a landmark day.

Nine

Alice was back in her office the following week. She'd turned the thermos from the river in Jacobsville over to Longfellow first thing in the morning. She was waiting for results, going over a case file, when the door opened and a tall, distinguished-looking gentleman in an expensive dark blue suit walked in, unannounced. He had black hair with silver at the temples, and light blue eyes. She recognized him at once.

"Senator Fowler," she said quietly.

"Ms. Jones," he replied. He stood over the desk with his hands in his pockets. "I wonder if you could spare me a few minutes?"

"Of course." She indicated the chair in front of her desk.

He took his hands out of his pockets and sat down,

crossing one long leg over the other. "I believe you know my son."

She smiled. "Yes. I know Harley."

"I... My wife and I haven't seen him for many years," he began. "We made terrible mistakes. Now, it seems that we'll never be able to find our way back to him. He's grown into a fine-looking young man. He... has a job?"

She nodded. "A very good one. And friends."

"I'm glad. I'm very glad." He hesitated. "We didn't know how to cope with him. He was such a cocky young-ster, so sure that he had all the answers." He looked down at his shoes. "We should have been kinder."

"You lost your daughter," Alice said very gently.

He lifted his eyes and they shimmered with pain and grief. "I killed...my daughter," he gritted. "Backed over her with my car rushing to get to a campaign rally." He closed his eyes. "Afterward, I went mad."

"So did your wife, I think," Alice said quietly.

He nodded. He brushed at his eyes and averted them. "She was a superior court judge. She started drinking and quit the bench. She said she couldn't sit in judgment on other people when her own mistakes were so terrible. She was on the phone when it happened. She'd just told our daughter, Cecily, to stop interrupting her and go away. You know, the sort of offhand remark parents make. It doesn't mean they don't love the child. Anyway, Cecily sneaked out the door and went behind the car, un-beknownst to me, apparently to get a toy she'd tossed under it. I jumped in without looking to see if there was anybody behind me. I was late getting to a meeting... Anyway, my wife never knew Cecily was outside until I started screaming, when I knew what I'd done." He leaned forward. "We blamed each other. We had fights. Harley grieved. He blamed me, most of all. But he seemed to just get right on with his life afterward."

"I don't think any of you did that," Alice replied. "I don't think you dealt with it."

He looked up. His blue eyes were damp. "How do you know so much?"

"I deal with death every day," she said simply. "I've seen families torn apart by tragedies. Very few people admit that they need help, or get counseling. It is horrible to lose a child. It's traumatic to lose one the way you did. You should have been in therapy, all of you."

"I wasn't the sort of person who could have admitted that," he said simply. "I was more concerned with my image. It was an election year, you see. I threw myself into the campaign and thought that would accomplish the same thing. So did my wife." He shook his head. "She decided to start a business, to keep busy." He managed a smile. "Now we never see each other. After Harley left, we blamed each other for that, too."

She studied the older man curiously. "You're a politician. You must have access to investigators. You could have found Harley any time you wanted to."

He hesitated. Then he nodded. "But that works both ways, Ms. Jones. He could have found us, too. We didn't move around."

"Harley said you wanted him to be part of a social set that he didn't like."

"Do you think I like it?" he asked suddenly and gave a bitter laugh. "I love my job. I have power. I can do a lot of good, and I do. But socializing is part of that job. I do more business at cocktail parties than I've ever done in my office in Washington. I make contacts, I get networks going, I research. I never stop." He sighed. "I tried to explain that to Harley, but he thought I meant that I wanted to use him to reel in campaign workers." He laughed. "It's funny now. He was so green, so naive. He thought he knew all there was to know about politics and life." He looked up. "I hope he's learned that nothing is black or white."

"He's learned a lot," she replied. "But he's been running away from his past for years."

"Too many years. I can't approach him directly. He'd take off." He clasped his hands together. "I was hoping you might find it in your heart to pave the way for me. Just a little. I only want to talk to him."

She narrowed her eyes. "This wouldn't have anything to do with the woman we talked to at your fundraising party…?"

He stared at her with piercing blue eyes just a shade lighter than Harley's. "You're very quick."

"I didn't start this job yesterday," she replied, and smiled faintly.

He drew in a long breath. "I gave Dolores a hard time. She was deeply religious, but she got on my nerves. A man who's forsaken religion doesn't like sermons," he added, laughing bitterly. "But she was a good person. My wife had a heart attack earlier this year. I hired a nurse to sit with her, when she got home from the hospital. Unknown to me, the nurse drugged my wife and left the house to party with her boyfriend. Dolores made sure I found out. Then she sat with my wife. They found a lot to talk about. After my wife got back on her feet, she began to change for the better. I think it was Dolores's influence." He hung his head. "I was harsh to Dolores the night of the fundraiser. That's haunted me, too. I have a young protégé, our newest senator. He's got a brother who makes me very nervous…" He lifted his eyes. "Sorry. I keep getting off the track. I do want you to help me reconnect with my son, if you can. But that's not why I'm here."

"Then why are you here, Senator?" she asked.

He looked her in the eye. "Dolores didn't commit suicide."

Her heart jumped, but she kept a straight face. She linked her hands in front of her on the desk and leaned forward. "Why do you think that?"

"Because once, when I was despondent, I made a joke about running my car into a tree. She was eloquent on the subject of suicide. She thought it was the greatest sin of all. She said that it was an insult to God and it caused so much grief for people who loved you." He looked up. "I'm not an investigator, but I know she was right-handed. She was shot in the right side of her body." He shook his head. "She wasn't the sort of person to do that. She hated guns. I'm sure she never owned one. It doesn't feel right."

"I couldn't force the assistant medical examiner to write it up as a homicide. He's near retirement, and it was your employee who died. He's afraid of you, of your influence. He knows that you stopped the investigation on the Kilraven case stone-cold."

"I didn't," he said unexpectedly, and his mouth tightened. "Will Sanders is the new junior senator from Texas," he continued. "He's a nice guy, but his brother is a small-time hoodlum with some nasty contacts, who mixes with dangerous people. He's involved in illegal enterprises. Will can't stop him, but he does try to protect him. Obviously he thinks Hank knows something about the Kilraven case, and he doesn't want it discovered."

Alice's blue eyes began to glitter. "Murder is a nasty business," she pointed out. "Would you like to know what was done to Kilraven's wife and three-year-old daughter?" she added. "He saw it up close, by accident. But I have autopsy photos that I've never shown anyone, if you'd like to see what happened to them."

The senator paled. "I would not," he replied. He stared into space. "I'm willing for Kilraven to look into the case. Rick Marquez's colleague was sent to work in traffic control. I'm sorry for that. Will persuaded me to get her off the case. She's a bulldog when it comes to homicide investigation, and she stops at nothing to solve a crime." He looked up. "Will's rather forceful in his way. I let him lead me sometimes. But I don't want either of us being shown as obstructing a murder investigation, even one that's seven years old. He's probably afraid that his brother, Hank, may have knowledge of the perpetrator and Will's trying to shield him. He's done that all his life. But he has no idea what the media would do to him if it ever came out that he'd hindered the discovery of a murderer, especially in a case as horrific as this."

"I've seen what happens when people conceal evidence. It's not pretty," Alice said. "How can you help Kilraven?"

"For one thing, I can smooth the way for Marquez's colleague. I'll go have a talk with the police commissioner when I leave here. He'll get her reassigned to Homicide. Here." He scribbled a number on a piece of paper and handed it to her. "That's my private cell number. I keep two phones on me, but only a few people have access to this number. Tell Kilraven to call me. Or do you have his number?"

"Sure." She pulled out her own cell phone, pushed a few buttons and wrote down Kilraven's cell phone number on a scrap of paper. Odd, how familiar that number looked on paper. She handed it to the senator. "There."

"Thanks. Uh, if you like," he added with a smile as he stood up, "you could share my private number with Harley. He can call me anytime. Even if I'm standing at a podium making a speech somewhere. I won't mind being interrupted."

She stood up, too, smiling. "I'm going down there Wednesday for the New Year's Eve celebration in town, as it happens, with Harley. I'll pass it along. Thanks, Senator Fowler."

He shook hands with her. "If I can pave the way for you in the investigation into Dolores's death, I'll be glad to," he added.

"I'll keep you in mind. Kilraven will be grateful for your help, I'm sure."

He smiled, waved and left.

Alice sat down. Something wasn't right. She pulled up her notes on the Jacobsville murder investigation and scrolled down to the series of numbers that Longfellow had transcribed from the piece of paper in the victim's hand. Gasping, she pulled up Kilraven's cell phone number on her own cell phone and compared them. The digits that were decipherable were a match for everything except the area code, which was missing. It wasn't conclusive, but it was pretty certain that the murder victim had come to contact Kilraven. Which begged the question, did the victim know something about the old murder case?

Her first instinct was to pick up the phone and call Kilraven. But her second was caution. Without the missing numbers, it could be a coincidence. Better to let the senator call Kilraven and get him some help—Marquez's detective friend—and go from there. Meanwhile, Alice would press Longfellow about the faded, wet portion of the paper where the first few numbers were, so far, unreadable. The FBI lab had the technology enabling them to pull up the faintest traces of ink. They might work a miracle for the investigation.

The thermos contained a tiny residue of coffee laced with a narcotic drug, Longfellow told Alice. "If it's connected to your case," the assistant investigator told Alice, "it could explain a lot. It would make the victim less able to defend himself from an attacker."

"Fingerprints?"

Longfellow shook her head. "It was clean. Wiped, apparently, and just tossed away. It's as if," she added, frowning, "the killer was so confident that he left the thermos deliberately, to show his superiority."

Alice smiled faintly. "I love it when perps do that," she said. "When we catch them, and get them into court, that cockiness usually takes a nosedive. It's a kick to see it."

"Indeed," Longfellow added. "I'll keep digging, though," she assured Alice.

"You do that. We'll need every scrap of evidence we have to pin this murder on somebody. The killer's good. Very good." She frowned. "He's probably done this before and never got caught."

"That might explain his efficiency," the other woman agreed. "But he missed that scrap of paper in the victim's hand."

"Every criminal slips up eventually. Let's hope this is his swan song."

"Oh, yes."

Alice drove down to Jacobsville in her personal car, a little Honda with terrific gas mileage, and checked in at the motel. She'd reserved a room, to make sure she got one, because out-of-town people came for the New Year's Eve celebration. Once she was checked in, she phoned Harley.

"I was going to come up and get you," he protested.

"I don't want you on the roads at night, either, Harley," she replied softly.

He sighed. "What am I going to do with you, Alice?"

"I have several suggestions," she began brightly.

He laughed. "You can tell me tonight. Barbara's Café is staying open for the festivities. Suppose I come and get you about six, and we'll have supper. Then we'll go to the Cattlemen's Association building where the party's being held."

"That sounds great."

"It's formal," he added hesitantly.

"No worries. I brought my skimpy little black cocktail dress and my sassy boa."

He chuckled. "Not a live one, I hope."

"Nope."

"I'll see you later, then," he said in a low, sexy tone.

"I'll look forward to it."

He hung up. So did she. Then she checked her watch. It was going to be a long afternoon.

Harley caught his breath when she opened the door. She was dressed in a little black silk dress with spaghetti straps and a brief, low-cut bodice that made the most of her pert breasts. The dress clung to her hips and fell to her knees in silky profusion. She wore dark hose and black slingback pumps. She'd used enough makeup to give her an odd, foreign appearance. Her lips, plumped with glossy red stay-on lipstick, were tempting. She wore a knitted black boa with blue feathery wisps and carried a small black evening bag with a long strap.

"Will I do?" Alice asked innocently.

Harley couldn't even speak. He nudged her back into the room, closed and locked the door, took off his hat and his jacket and pushed her gently onto the bed.

"Sorry," he murmured as his mouth took hers like a whirlwind.

She moaned as he slid onto her, teasing her legs apart so that he could ease up her skirt and touch the soft flesh there with a lean, exploring hand.

His mouth became demanding. His hands moved up and down her yielding body, discovering soft curves and softer flesh beneath. With his mouth still insistent on her parting lips, he brushed away the spaghetti straps and bared her to the waist. He lifted his head to look at her taut, mauve-tipped breasts. "Beautiful," he whispered, and his mouth diverted to the hardness, covered it delicately, and with a subtle suction that arched her off the bed in a stab of pleasure so deep that it seemed to make her swell all over.

She forced his head closer, writhing under him as the hunger built and built in the secret silence of the room. All she wanted was for him never to stop. She whispered it, moaning, coaxing, as the flames grew higher and higher, and his hands reached under her, searching for a waistband...

Her cell phone blared out the theme from the original *Indiana Jones* movie. They both jumped at the sound. Harley, his mind returning to normal, quickly drew his hands out from under Alice's skirt with a grimace, and rolled away. He lay struggling to get his breath while she eased off the bed and retrieved her purse from the floor, where she'd dropped it.

"Jones," she managed in a hoarse tone.

"Alice?" Hayes Carson asked, because she didn't sound like herself.

"Yes," she said, forcing herself to breathe normally. "Hayes?"

"Yes. I wanted to know if you found out anything about that thermos." He hesitated. "Did I call at a bad time?"

She managed a laugh. "We could debate that," she said. "Actually the thermos was clean. No fingerprints, but the liquid in it had traces of a narcotic laced in it," she replied. "But Longfellow's still looking. We've got the note at the FBI lab. Hopefully they'll be able to get the missing numbers for us. But they've got a backlog and it's the holidays. Not much hope for anything this week."

"I was afraid of that."

"Well, we live in hope," she said, and glanced at Harley, who was now sitting up and looking pained.

"We do. Coming to the celebration tonight?"

"Sure am. You coming?"

"I never miss it. Uh, is Harley bringing you?"

She laughed. "He is. We'll see you there."

"Sure thing." He hung up.

She glanced at Harley with a wicked smile. "Well, we can think of Hayes as portable birth control tonight, can't we?"

He burst out laughing despite his discomfort. He managed to get to his feet, still struggling to breathe normally. "I can think of a few other pertinent adjectives that would fit him."

"Unprintable ones, I'll bet." She went up to him and put her hands on his broad chest. She reached up to kiss him softly. "It was good timing. I couldn't have stopped."

"Yeah. Me, neither," he confessed, flushing a little. "It's been a long dry spell." He bent and brushed his mouth over hers. "But we've proven that we're physically compatible," he mused.

"Definitely." She pursed her lips. "So how about we get married tomorrow morning?"

He chuckled. "Can't. I'm brushing bulls for a regional show."

"Brushing bulls?" she wondered aloud.

"Purebred herd sires. They have to be brushed and combed and dolled up. The more ribbons we win, the higher we can charge for their, uh, well, for straws."

Of semen, he meant, but he was too nice to say it bluntly. "I know what straws are, Harley." She grinned. "I get the idea."

"So not tomorrow."

"I live in hope," she returned. She went to the mirror in the bathroom to repair her makeup, which was royally smeared. "Better check your face, too," she called. "This never-smear lipstick has dishonest publicity. It does smear."

He walked up behind her. His shirt was undone. She remembered doing that, her hands buried in the thick hair that covered his chest, tugging it while he kissed her. She flushed at the memory.

He checked his face, decided it would pass, and lowered his eyes to Alice's flushed cheeks in the mirror. He put his hands on her shoulders and tightened them. "We can't get married tomorrow. But I thought, maybe next week. Friday, maybe," he said softly. "I can take a few days off. We could drive down to Galveston. To the beach. Even in winter, it's beautiful there."

She'd turned and was staring up at him wide-eyed. "You mean that? It isn't you're just saying it so I'll stop harassing you?"

He bent and kissed her forehead with breathless tenderness. "I don't know how it happened, exactly," he said in a husky, soft tone. "But I'm in love with you."

She slid her arms around his neck. "I'm in love with you, too, Harley," she said in a wondering tone, searching his eyes.

He lifted her up to him and kissed her in a new way, a different way. With reverence, and respect, and aching tenderness.

"I'll marry you whenever you like," she said against his mouth.

He kissed her harder. The passion returned, riveting them together, locking them in a heat of desire that was ever more formidable to resist.

He drew back, grinding his teeth in frustration, and moved her away from him. "We have to stop this," he said. "At least until after the wedding. I'm really old-fashioned about these things."

"Tell me about it," she said huskily. "I come from a whole family of Baptist ministers. Need I say more?"

He managed a smile. "No. I know what you mean." He drew a steadying breath and looked in the mirror. He grimaced. "Okay, now I believe that publicity was a load of bull," he told her. "I'm smeared, too, and it's not my color."

"It definitely isn't," she agreed. She wet a washcloth and proceeded to clean up both of them. Then, while he got his suit coat back on, and his hair combed, she finished her own makeup. By the time she was done, he was waiting for her at the door. He smiled as she approached him.

"You look sharp," he said gently.

She whirled the boa around her neck and smiled from ear to ear. "You look devastating," she replied.

He stuck out an arm. She linked her hand into it. He opened the door and followed her out.

There was a band. They played regional favorites, and Harley danced with Alice. Practically the whole town had gathered in the building that housed the local Cattlemen's Association, to celebrate the coming of the new year. A pair of steer horns, the idea of Calhoun Ballenger, their new state senator, waited to fall when midnight came.

Hayes Carson was wearing his uniform, and Alice teased him about it.

"Hey, I'm on duty," he replied with a grin. "And I'm only here between calls."

"I'm not arguing. It's a big turnout. Is it always like this?"

"Always," Hayes replied. He started to add to that when a call came over his radio. He pressed the button on his portable and told the dispatcher he was en route to the call. "See what I mean?" he added with a sigh. "Have fun."

"We will," Harley replied, sliding an arm around her.

Hayes waved as he went out the door.

"Is he sweet on you?" Harley asked with just a hint of jealousy in his tone.

She pressed close to him. "Everybody but Hayes knows that he's sweet on Minette Raynor, but he's never going to admit it. He's spent years blaming her for his younger brother's drug-related death. She wasn't responsible, and he even knows who was because there was a confession."

"That's sad," Harley replied.

"It is." She looked up at him and smiled. "But it's not our problem. You said we'd get married next Friday. I'll have to ask for time off."

He pursed his lips. "So will I. Do you want to get married in church?"

She hesitated. "Could we?"

"Yes. I'll make the arrangements. What sort of flowers do you want, for your bouquet?"

"Yellow and white roses," she said at once. "But, Harley, I don't have a wedding gown. You don't want a big reception?"

"Not very big, no, but you should have a wedding gown," he replied solemnly. "If we have a daughter, she could have it for her own wedding one day. Or it could be an heirloom, at least, to hand down."

"A daughter. Children..." She caught her breath. "I hadn't thought about... Oh, yes, I want children! I want them so much!"

His body corded. "So do I."

"I'll buy a wedding gown, first thing when I get home," she said. "I'll need a maid of honor. You'll need a best man," she added quickly.

"I'll ask Mr. Parks," he said.

She smiled. "I don't really have many women friends. Do you suppose Mrs. Parks would be my matron of honor?"

"I think she'd be honored," Harley replied. "I'll ask them."

"Wow," she said softly. "It's all happening so fast." She frowned. "Not too fast, is it?" she worried aloud.

"Not too fast," he assured her. "We're the same sort of people, Alice. We'll fit together like a puzzle. I promise you we will. I'll take care of you all my life."

"I'll take care of you," she replied solemnly. "I want to keep my job."

He smiled. "Of course you do. You can commute, can't you?"

She smiled. "Of course. I have a Honda."

"I've seen it. Nice little car. I've got a truck, so we can haul stuff. Mr. Parks is giving me some land and some cattle from his purebred herd. There's an old house on the land. It's not the best place to set up housekeeping, but Mr. Parks said the minute I proposed, to let him know and he'd get a construction crew out there to remodel it." He hesitated. "I told him Saturday that I was going to propose to you."

Her lips parted. "Saturday?"

He nodded. "That's when I knew I couldn't live without you, Alice."

She pressed close into his arms, not caring what anybody thought. "I felt that way, too. Like I've always known you."

He kissed her forehead and held her tight. "Yes. So we have a place to live. The boss will have it in great shape when we get back from our honeymoon." He lifted his head. "Will you mind living on a ranch?"

"Are you kidding? I want to keep chickens and learn to can and make my own butter."

He laughed. "Really?"

"Really! I hate living in the city. I can't even keep a cat in my apartment, much less grow things there." She beamed. "I'll love it!"

He grinned back. "I'll bring you one of my chicken catalogs. I like the fancy ones, but you can get regular hens as well."

"Chicken catalogs? You like chickens?"

"Boss keeps them," he said. "I used to gather eggs for Mrs. Parks, years ago. I like hens. I had my mind on a small ranch and I thought chickens would go nicely with cattle."

She sighed. "We're going to be very happy, I think."

"I think so, too."

The Parkses showed up, along with the Steeles and the Scotts. Harley and Alice announced their plans, and the Parkses agreed with delightful speed to take part in the wedding. Other local citizens gathered around to congratulate them.

Midnight came all too soon. The steer horns lowered to the loud count by the crowd, out under the bright Texas stars to celebrate the new year. The horns made it to the ground, the band struck up "Auld Lang Syne" and everybody kissed and cried and threw confetti.

"Happy New Year, Alice," Harley whispered as he bent to kiss her.

"Happy New Year." She threw her arms around him and kissed him back.

He left her at her motel with real reluctance. "I won't come in," he said at once, grinning wickedly. "We've already discovered that I have no willpower."

"Neither do I," she sighed. "I guess we're very

strange. Most people who get married have been living together for years. We're the odd couple, waiting until after the ceremony."

He became serious. "It all goes back to those old ideals, to the nobility of the human spirit," he said softly. "Tradition is important. And I love the idea of chastity. I'm only sorry that I didn't wait for you, Alice. But, then, I didn't know you were going to come along. I'd decided that I'd never find someone I wanted to spend my life with." He smiled. "What a surprise you were."

She went close and hugged him. "You're the nicest man I've ever known. No qualms about what I do for a living?" she added.

He shrugged. "It's a job. I work with cattle and get sunk up to my knees in cow manure. It's not so different from what you do. We both get covered up in disgusting substances to do our jobs."

"I never thought of it like that."

He hugged her close. "We'll get along fine. And we'll wait, even if half the world thinks we're nuts."

"Speaking for myself, I've always been goofy."

"So have I."

"Besides," she said, pulling back, "I was never one to go with the crowd. You'll call me?"

"Every day," he said huskily. "A week from Friday."

She smiled warmly. "A week from Friday. Happy New Year."

He kissed her. "Happy New Year."

He got back into his car. He didn't drive away until she was safely inside her room.

Ten

Alice had forgotten, in the excitement, to tell Harley about the senator's message. But the following day, when he called, he didn't have time to talk. So she waited until Friday, when he phoned and was in a chatty mood,

"I have a message for you," she said hesitantly. "From your father."

"My father?" he said after a minute, and he was solemn.

"He said that he'd made some dreadful mistakes. He wants the opportunity to apologize for them. Your sister's death caused problems for both your parents that they never faced."

"Yes, and I never realized it. When did you talk to him?"

"He came to see me Monday, at my office. I like him," she added quietly. "I think he was sincere, about wanting to reconnect with you. He gave me his private cell phone number." She hesitated. "Do you want it?"

He hesitated, too, but only for a moment. "Yes."

She called out the numbers to him.

"I'm not saying I'll call him," he said after a minute. "But I'll think about it."

"That's my guy," she replied, and felt warm all over at the thought. She'd had some worries, though. "Harley?"

"Hmm?"

"You know that we've only known each other for a few weeks…" she began.

"And you're afraid we're rushing into marriage?"

She shrugged. "Aren't we?"

He laughed softly. "Alice, we can wait for several months or several years, but in the end, we'll get married. We have so much in common that no sane gambler would bet against us. But if you want to wait, honey, we'll wait." He cleared his throat. "It's just that my willpower may not be up to it. Just don't expect to get married in a white gown, okay?"

She remembered their close calls and laughed. "Okay, I'm convinced. We'll get married a week from Friday."

"Wear a veil, will you," he added seriously. "It's old-fashioned, but it's so beautiful."

"Say no more. I'll shop veils-are-us this very day."

"There's such a place?" he asked.

"I'll let you know."

"Deal. I'll call you tonight."

She felt a flush of warmth. "Okay."

"Bye, darlin'," he drawled, and hung up.

Alice held the phone close, sighing, until Longfellow walked by and gave her a strange look.

Alice removed the phone from her chest and put it

carefully on the desk. "Magnetism, Longfellow," she said facetiously. "You see, a burst of magnetism caught my cell phone and riveted it to my chest. I have only just managed to extricate it." She waited hopefully for the reply.

Longfellow pursed her lips. "You just stick to that story, but I have reason to know that you have recently become engaged. So I'll bet your boyfriend just hung up."

"Who told you I was engaged?" Alice demanded.

Longfellow started counting them off on her fingers. "Rick Marquez, Jon Blackhawk, Kilraven, Hayes Carson…"

"How do you know Kilraven?" Alice wanted to know.

"He keeps bugging me about that telephone number," she sighed. "As if the FBI lab doesn't have any other evidence to process. Give me a break!" She rolled her eyes.

"If they call you, get in touch with me before you tell Kilraven anything, okay?" she asked. "I want to make sure he's not running off into dead ends on my account."

"I'll do that," Longfellow promised. She stared at Alice. "If you want to shop for a wedding gown, I know just the place. And I'll be your fashion consultant."

Alice looked dubious.

"Wait a sec," Longfellow said. "I have photos of my own wedding, three years ago." She pulled them up on her phone and showed them to Alice. "That's my gown."

Alice caught her breath. "Where in the world did you find such a gown?"

"At a little boutique downtown, would you believe it? They do hand embroidery—although in your case, it will probably have to be machined—and they have a pretty good selection for a small shop."

"Can we go after work?" Alice asked enthusiastically.

Longfellow laughed. "You bet."

"Thanks."

"Not a problem."

Alice picked out a dream of a gown, white satin with delicate pastel silk embroidery on the hem in yellow and pink and blue. There was a long illusion veil that matched it, with just the ends embroidered delicately in silk in the same pastel colors. It wasn't even that expensive.

"Why aren't you on the news?" Alice asked the owner, a petite little brunette. "I've never seen such beautiful wedding gowns!"

"We don't appeal to everybody," came the reply. "But for the few, we're here."

"I'll spread the word around," Alice promised.

"I already have." Longfellow chuckled.

Outside the shop, with her purchase safely placed in the backseat of her car, Alice impulsively hugged Longfellow. "Thanks so much."

"It was my pleasure," Longfellow replied. "Where will you live?"

"He's got a small ranch," she said proudly. "We're going to raise purebred Santa Gertrudis cattle. But until we make our first million at it, he's going to go on working as a ranch foreman, and I'll keep my job here. I'll commute."

"You always wanted to live in the country," Longfellow recalled.

Alice smiled. "Yes. And with the right man. I have definitely found him." She sighed. "I know it sounds like a rushed thing. We've known each other just a short time…"

"My sister met her husband and got married in five

days," Longfellow said smugly. "They just celebrated their thirty-seventh wedding anniversary."

"Thirty-seven years?" Alice exclaimed.

"Well, he liked *Star Trek,* she said," Longfellow explained. "She said that told her everything she needed to know about him—that he was intelligent, tolerant, inquisitive, optimistic about the future, unprejudiced and a little quirky." She shrugged and laughed. "Not bad for a quick character reading, was it?"

"Not at all. Good for her!"

"You do the same," Longfellow lectured. "I don't want to see you in divorce court a month after you say your vows."

"I believe we can safely say that won't happen," Alice replied, and she felt and sounded confident. She frowned. "I wonder if he likes *Star Trek,*" she wondered aloud.

In fact, she asked him when he called that night. "I do," he replied. "All the series, all the movies, and especially the new one, about Kirk, Spock and McCoy as cadets." He paused. "How about you?"

"I love it, too." She laughed, and then explained why she'd asked the question.

He was serious then. "That's a long time," he said of Longfellow's sister's marriage. "We'll give her a run for her money, won't we, Alice?"

She smiled. "Yes, we will."

There was a long pause. "You're wondering if I called that number you gave me," Harley said.

She laughed in surprise. "You read minds! That's great! If we ever have an argument, you'll know why I was mad and just what to do about it!"

"I only read minds occasionally," he told her, "so

let's not have arguments. But I did call my father. We had a long talk. I think we may get together one day, with my mother, and try to iron things out."

"That's wonderful," she said softly.

"It won't be easy to get over the past, but at least we're all willing to try. I did mention the wedding to him."

"And?"

"He said that if he showed up, we'd be a media lunch. I have to agree," he added. "I don't want that. Neither do you. But we're invited to their house for a potluck dinner the day we get back from our honeymoon."

"I'd enjoy that."

"Me, too."

"I bought a wedding gown. With a veil. It's beautiful."

"On you, any gown would be. You're delicious, Alice."

She laughed softly. "That's just the right thing to say."

"I mean it, too."

"I know."

"Game for a movie tomorrow night?" he asked. "There's a Christmas-themed one we could go see."

"That would be fun. Yes."

"I'll pick you up at six and we'll have supper first."

"That's a date."

"Uh, and no stopping by your apartment after. I go home."

"Yes, Harley. You go home."

There was a brief pause and they both burst out laughing.

He did go home, but only after a heated session on her sofa that ended with him actually pulling away and running for the door. He waved as he slammed it behind him, leaving a disheveled Alice laughing her head off.

* * *

It was raining on their wedding day. Alice carried an umbrella over her gown and Lisa Parks held up the train as they rushed into the church just ahead of a thunderbolt. Cy Parks was waiting at the altar with Harley, who looked devastating in a tuxedo, a conventional black one with a white shirt and black bow tie. Harley couldn't take his eyes off Alice.

Lisa went to her seat. The full church quieted. Alice smiled as the Wedding March struck up on the organ and she adjusted her train before she picked up the pretty bouquet he'd ordered for her. The fingertip veil just hid the wetness in her eyes as she wished with all her heart that her parents had been here to see her marry.

She walked slowly down the aisle, aware of friendly, curious eyes admiring her dress. Leo Hart and his wife, Janie, were sitting on the aisle. Alice didn't know, but Janie had dated Harley while she was trying to get over Leo. It hadn't been serious. In fact, Harley had dated several local women, including one who'd cast him off like a wet shoe and hurt his pride. It had seemed to many people as if Harley would always be the stand-in for some other man. But here he was with a really pretty, professional woman, and she had a reputation as a keen investigator. Many people in Jacobsville watched the crime scene investigation shows. They grinned as they considered how nice it was going to be, having somebody local who could answer all those questions they wanted to ask about homicide investigation.

Alice paused at the altar, looked up at Harley and felt a moment of panic. They hardly knew each other. They were almost strangers. This was insane…!

Just then, as if he knew what she was feeling,

Harley's big hand reached over and linked itself unob-
trusively into her cold fingers and pressed them, very
gently. She looked into his eyes. He was smiling, with
love and pride and confidence. All at once, she relaxed
and smiled back.

The minister cleared his throat.

"Sorry," Alice mouthed, and turned her attention to
him instead of Harley.

The minister, who had a daughter just Alice's age,
grinned at her and began the service.

It was brief, but poignant. At the end of it, Harley
lifted the exquisite veil and kissed his bride. Alice
fought back tears as she returned the tender kiss.

They ran out of the church amid a shower of confetti
and well wishes.

"Good thing you aren't having a reception," Cash
Grier remarked as they waited for the limousine Cy
Parks had ordered to take them to the airport, one of
several wedding presents.

"A reception?" Alice asked, curious. "Why?"

"Our local district attorney, Blake Kemp, had one,"
Cash explained. "He and his wife went home instead to
dress for their honeymoon. While they were gone, there
was an altercation. One of my officers was wearing the
punch, another salvaged just the top layer of the
wedding cake and most of the guests went to jail." He
grinned. "Jacobsville weddings are interesting."

They both laughed, and agreed that it was probably
a good thing after all.

Cy Parks paused with Lisa when the limo drove up
and the driver came around to open the rear door.

Cy shook hands with Harley. "Your house will be ready
when you get back," he told Harley. "You did good."

Harley beamed. "You'll never know how much it meant to me, that you and Lisa stood up with us. Thanks."

Cy was somber. "You're a good man, Harley. I hope my sons will be like you."

Harley had to bite down hard. "Thanks," he managed.

"Go have a nice honeymoon," Cy told the couple. He grinned. "I won't let the Hart boys near your house, either."

"The Hart boys?" Alice parroted.

Leo Hart leaned over her shoulder. "We have a reputation for making weddings interesting," he told her, and grinned.

"Not so much these days." Janie grinned from beside him.

A tall, silver-eyed man in a police uniform walked up beside them. Kilraven. Grinning. "I'm giving the limo a police escort to the airport," he told them.

"That's very nice of you," Alice told him.

He sighed. "Might as well, since there's no reception. Weddings are getting really somber around here."

"Why don't you get married and have a reception?" Cash Grier suggested.

Kilraven gave him a look. "And have women throwing themselves over cliffs because I went out of circulation? In your dreams, Grier!"

Everybody laughed.

Corpus Christi was a beautiful little city on the Gulf of Mexico. It had a sugar-sand beach and seagulls and a myriad of local shops with all sorts of souvenirs and pretty things to buy. Harley and Alice never noticed.

They'd managed to get checked in and they looked out the window at the beach. Then they looked at each other.

Clothes fell. Buttons popped. Intimate garments went everywhere. Alice threw back the covers and dived in just a few seconds ahead of her brand-new husband. In a tangle of arms and legs, they devoured each other in a surging crescendo of passion that lasted for what seemed hours.

"What are you waiting for?" Alice groaned. "Come back here!"

"I was only...trying to make it easier..." he began.

"Easier, the devil!" She arched up, grimacing, because it really did hurt. But only for a few seconds. She stiffened, but then the fever burned right back up again, and she dragged him down with a kiss that knocked every single worry right out of his mind.

"Oh, wow," she managed when the room stopped spinning around them. She was lying half under Harley, covered in sweat even in the cool room, shivering with delight. "Now that was a first time to write about!" she enthused.

He laughed. "I was trying not to hurt you," he pointed out.

She pushed him over and rolled onto him. "And I appreciate every single effort, but it wasn't necessary," she murmured as she kissed him. "I was starving for you!"

"I noticed."

She lifted up and gave him a wicked look.

"I was starving for you, too," he replied diplomatically, and chuckled. "You were incredible."

"So were you." She sighed and laid her cheek on his broad, hairy chest. "No wonder people don't wait for wedding nights anymore."

"Some of them do."

"It isn't night, yet," she reminded him.

He laughed softly. "I guess not."

She kissed his chest. "Should we go down to the restaurant to eat?"

"Mr. Parks gave us a one-week honeymoon with room service. I do not think we should insult the man by not using it," he replied.

"Oh, I do agree. I would hate to insult Mr. Parks. Besides," she murmured, shifting, "I just thought of something we can do to pass the time until supper!"

"You did?" He rolled her over, radiant. "Show me!"

She did.

They arrived home bleary-eyed from lack of sleep and with only a few photos and souvenirs of where they'd been. In actuality, they'd hardly seen anything except the ceiling of their hotel room.

The ranch house was one level. It was old, but well-kept, and it had new steps and porch rails, and a porch swing. It also had a new coat of white paint.

"It's just beautiful," Alice enthused. "Harley, it looks like the house I lived in when I was a little girl, growing up in Floresville!"

"You grew up in Floresville?" he asked as he unlocked the door and opened it.

She looked up at him. "We don't know a lot about each other, do we? It will give us something to talk about when we calm down just a little."

He grinned and swept her up in his arms, to carry her into the house. "Don't hold your breath waiting for that to happen," he advised.

She smiled and kissed him.

He put her down in the living room. She sighed. "Oh, my," she said softly.

There were roses everywhere, vases full of them, in

every color. There were colorful afghans and two sweaters (his and hers), a big-screen color television set, a DVD player, an Xbox 360 gaming system and several games, and a basket of fruit. On the dining-room table, there were containers of breads and a propped-up note pointing to the refrigerator. It was full of cooked food. There was even a cake for dessert.

"Good grief," Harley whistled. He picked up the note and read it. "Congratulations and best wishes from the Scotts, the Parkses, the Steeles, all the Harts, and the Pendletons." He gaped at her. "The Pendletons! Jason Pendleton is a multimillionaire! I thought he was going to deck me in San Antonio…" He hesitated to tell his new wife that he'd tried to date Jason's stepsister Gracie, who was now Mrs. Pendleton. He chuckled. "Well, I guess he forgave me. His mother has a craft shop and she knits. I'll bet she made the afghans for us."

Alice fingered the delicate stitches. "I'll be still writing thank-you notes when our kids are in grammar school," she remarked. "Harley, you have so many friends. I never realized." She turned and smiled at him. "We're going to be so happy here."

He beamed. He opened his arms and Alice ran into them, to be held close and hugged.

"Are you hungry?" he asked.

She peered up at him and laughed. "We didn't get breakfast."

"And whose fault was that, Mrs. Fowler?" he teased.

"I said I was hungry, it just wasn't for food. Well, not then. I could eat," she added, peering past him at the cake on the table.

"So could I, and I noticed fried chicken in the fridge. It's my favorite."

"Mine, too," she agreed. "I don't cook much on the weekdays because I'm on call so often." She looked up at him worriedly.

"I can cook, Alice," he assured her, smiling. "And I will, when I need to."

"You're just the best husband," she sighed.

"Glad you think so." He chuckled. "Let's find some plates."

They watched television while they nibbled on all sorts of delicious things. It was a treat that they both liked the same sort of shows. But they didn't watch it for long. The trip back had been tiring, and in many ways, it had been a long week. They slept soundly.

The next day, Alice had to drive up to her office to check on what progress had been made into the murder investigation while Harley got back to work on the ranch. He had things to do, as well, not to mention getting his own present of purebred cattle fed and watered and settled before he went over to Mr. Parks's house to do his job.

Longfellow welcomed her at the door with a hug. "Did you have a nice trip?"

"Lovely," Alice assured her. "But it's good to get home. We had food and presents waiting for us like you wouldn't believe. Mr. Parks had Harley's house renovated and he actually gave him a small herd of purebred cattle for a wedding gift—not to mention the honeymoon trip. What a boss!"

Longfellow smiled. "Surprising, isn't it, how generous he is. Considering the line of work he used to be in, it's a miracle he survived to get married and have a family."

"Yes, I know what you mean," Alice replied. "Any word yet on that scrap of paper we sent to the FBI lab?"

She shook her head. "The holidays, you know, and we're not at the top of the line for quick results." She pursed her lips. "Didn't you once bribe people to get faster service?" she teased.

Alice laughed. "I did, but I don't think my new husband would appreciate it if I did that sort of thing now."

"Probably not."

"Anything on the woman who died at Senator Fowler's house?" Alice added.

Longfellow frowned. "Actually, the senator stopped by and left you a note. I think I put it in your middle desk drawer. He said you were going to be a terrific daughter-in-law... Oops, I'm not supposed to know that, am I?"

Alice's eyes widened. She hadn't considered that she was now the daughter-in-law of the senior senator from Texas. She sat down, hard. "Well, my goodness," she said breathlessly. "I hadn't thought about that."

"You'll have clout in high places, if you ever need it," the other woman said wickedly. "You can threaten people with him!"

Alice laughed. "You idiot."

"I'd threaten people with him," came the reply. She frowned. "Especially Jon Blackhawk," she added.

"What's Jon done to you?"

"He called me at home at midnight to ask if we had lab results back on that thermos that Sheriff Hayes gave you."

"Now why would he want to know about that?"

Longfellow's eyes sparkled. "The investigator who was working with Marquez on the Kilraven case re-called seeing one like it."

"Where? When?"

"At the home of her ex-husband, actually," she said. "Remember that spiral design on the cup? It was rather odd, I thought at the time, like somebody had painted it with acrylics."

"Can we find out who her ex-husband is?" Alice asked excitedly.

"I did. He died a few weeks ago. The woman he was living with couldn't tell her anything about his friends or visitors, or about the thermos. The investigator told me that the woman was so strung out on coke that she hardly knew where she was."

"Pity," Alice replied sadly.

"Yes, and apparently the ex-husband had a drug problem of his own. Poor woman," she added softly. "She worked her way up to sergeant in the homicide division, and lost her promotion when she helped Marquez reopen the Kilraven cold case files."

Alice was only half listening now. She recalled the note the senator had left, pulled it out, opened it and read it. He'd talked to the police commissioner, he wrote, who had promised the reinstatement of the investigator on the Kilraven case. He'd also spoken to his colleague, the junior senator, and informed him that they were not going to try to hinder any murder investigations, regardless of how old they were. He'd talked to the coroner as well, and the autopsy on the senator's kitchen worker had been reclassified as a homicide. He hoped this would help. He reminded her that she and Harley should call and let them know when they were coming to supper. They had a wedding gift to present.

Alice whistled softly. "He's been busy." She told Longfellow the results of the senator's intercession. "What a nice man."

"Lucky you, to be related to him." The other woman chuckled. "See, I told you that… Wait a sec."

Her phone was ringing. She picked it up, raised her eyebrows at Alice and pulled a pen and paper toward her. "That's very nice of you! We didn't expect to hear back so soon. Yes, I'm ready. Yes." She was writing. She nodded. "I've got it. Yes. Yes, that will be fine. Thank you!" She hung up. "The FBI lab!" she exclaimed. "They've deciphered the rest of the numbers on that slip of paper you found in the victim's hand in Jacobsville!"

"Really? Let me see!"

Alice picked up the slip of paper and read the numbers with a sinking feeling in her stomach. Now there was no doubt, none at all, who the victim had come to Jacobsville to see. The number was for Kilraven's cell phone.

Eleven

Kilraven waited for Alice in the squad room at the Jacobsville Police Department. Alice had driven down in the middle of the day. She didn't want him to have to wait for the news, but she didn't want to tell him over the phone, either.

He stood up when she walked in and closed the door behind her. "Well?" he asked.

"The number on that slip of paper in the dead man's hand," she said. "It was your cell phone number."

He let out a breath. His eyes were sad and bitter. "He knew something about the murder. He came to tell me. Somebody knew or suspected, and they killed him."

"Then they figured that Dolores, who worked for Senator Fowler, might have heard something from the man, and they killed her, too. This is a nasty business."

"Very," Kilraven replied. "But this case is going to

break the older one," he added. "I'm sure of it. Thanks, Alice," he added quietly. "I owe you one."

"I'll remember that," she said, smiling. "Keep me in the loop, will you? Oh, there's another thing, I almost forgot. That thermos that Sheriff Hayes found, the one wiped clean of prints? Your investigator in San Antonio actually recognized it! It belonged to her ex-husband!"

"Oh, boy," he said heavily. "That's going to cause some pain locally."

"It is? Why?"

"Her ex-husband is the uncle of Winnie Sinclair."

"Does Winnie know?" Alice asked, stunned.

"No. And you can't tell her." His eyes had an odd, pained look. "I'll have to do it, somehow."

"Was he the sort of person who'd get mixed up in murder?"

"I don't know. But he's dead now. Whatever he knew died with him. Thanks again, Alice. I will keep you in the loop," he promised.

She nodded and he left her standing there. She felt his pain. Her own life was so blessed, she thought. Kilraven's was a study in anguish. Maybe he could solve the case at last, though. And maybe little Winnie Sinclair would have a happier future than she expected. Certainly, Kilraven seemed concerned about her feelings.

Alice and Harley went to supper with the senator and his wife. They were hesitant at first, with Harley, but as the evening wore on, they talked. Old wounds were reopened, but also lanced. By the time the younger Fowlers left, there was a détente.

"It went better than I expected it to," Harley said. "I suppose all three of us had unrealistic expectations."

She smiled. "They were proud of you when they heard what you'd done with your life. You could tell."

He smiled. "I grew up. I was such a cocky brat when I went to work for Cy Parks." He chuckled. "But I grew up fast. I learned a lot. I'm still learning." He glanced at her as he drove. "Nice presents they gave us, too. A little unexpected."

"Yes. A telescope." She glanced through the back window of the pickup at it, in its thick cardboard box, lying in the bed of the truck. "An eight-inch Schmidt-Cassegrain, at that," she mused.

He stood up on the brakes. "You know what it is?" he burst out.

"Oh, yes, I took a course in astronomy. I have volumes in my office on…" She stopped. The senator had been in her office. She laughed. "My goodness, he's observant!"

"My present isn't bad, either."

They'd given Harley a new saddle, a very ornate one that he could use while riding in parades. "Somebody must have told them what you were doing for a living while we were on our honeymoon," she guessed.

"My father is a digger." He laughed. "I'm sure he asked around."

"We have to spend time with them," she told him. "Family is important. Especially, when you don't have any left."

"You have uncles," he reminded her.

"Yes, but they all live far away and we were never close. I'd like very much to have children. And they'll need a granny and granddaddy, won't they?"

He reached across the seat and linked her hand into his. "Yes." He squeezed her fingers. "We're going to be happy, Alice."

She leaned her head back and stared at him with utter delight. "We're going to be very happy, Harley," she replied. She closed her eyes with a sigh, and smiled. "Very happy."

* * * * *

From glass slippers to silk sheets

Once upon a time there was a humble housekeeper.
Proud but poor, she went to work for a charming and
ruthless rich man!

She thought her place was below stairs—
but her gorgeous boss had other ideas.

Her place was in the bedroom, between his
luxurious silk sheets.

Stripped of her threadbare uniform, buxom and blushing
in his bed, she'll discover that a woman's work has never
been so much fun!

Look out for:

POWERFUL ITALIAN, PENNILESS HOUSEKEEPER

by India Grey

#2886

Available January 2010

New Year, New Man!

*For the perfect New Year's punch,
blend the following:*

- *One woman determined to find her inner vixen*
- *A notorious—and notoriously hot!—playboy*
- *A provocative New Year's Eve bash*
- *An impulsive kiss that leads to a night of
explosive passion!*

When the clock hits midnight Claire Daniels
kisses the guy standing closest to her, but
the kiss doesn't end after the bells stop ringing….

Look for

Moonstruck

by *USA TODAY* bestselling author

JULIE KENNER

Available January

---

red-hot reads

www.eHarlequin.com

Choose the romance that suits your reading mood

Passion

Harlequin Presents®
Intense and provocatively passionate love affairs set in glamorous international settings.

Silhouette Desire®
Rich, powerful heroes and scandalous family sagas.

Harlequin® Blaze™
Fun, flirtatious and steamy books that tell it like it is, inside and outside the bedroom.

Choose the romance that suits your reading mood

Suspense and Paranormal

Harlequin Intrigue®
Breathtaking romantic suspense.
Crime stories that will keep you
on the edge of your seat.

Silhouette® Romantic Suspense
Heart-racing sensuality and the
promise of a sweeping romance
set against the backdrop of
suspense.

Silhouette® Nocturne™
Dark and sensual paranormal
romance reads that stretch
the boundaries of conflict and
desire, life and death.

Choose the romance that suits your reading mood

Romance

Harlequin® Romance
The anticipation, the thrill of the chase and the sheer rush of falling in love!

Harlequin® Historical
Roguish rakes and rugged cowboys capture your imagination in these stories where chivalry still exists!

Harlequin's officially licensed NASCAR series
The rush of the professional race car circuit; the thrill of falling in love.